SIMON CHESTERMAN

RAISING ARCADIA

mc **Marshall Cavendish**
Editions

Cover design by Cover Kitchen
Illustrations by Ashley Penney
Author's photograph by Isabelle Delcourt
Book design by Benson Tan

Published by Marshall Cavendish Editions
An imprint of Marshall Cavendish International

Reprinted 2016, 2017

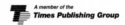

A member of the
Times Publishing Group

Other Marshall Cavendish Offices:
Marshall Cavendish Corporation. 99 White Plains Road, Tarrytown NY 10591-9001, USA • Marshall Cavendish International (Thailand) Co Ltd. 253 Asoke, 12th Flr, Sukhumvit 21 Road, Klongtoey Nua, Wattana, Bangkok 10110, Thailand • Marshall Cavendish (Malaysia) Sdn Bhd, Times Subang, Lot 46, Subang Hi-Tech Industrial Park, Batu Tiga, 40000 Shah Alam, Selangor Darul Ehsan, Malaysia

Marshall Cavendish is a registered trademark of Times Publishing Limited

National Library Board, Singapore Cataloguing-in-Publication Data

Name(s): Chesterman, Simon.
Title: Raising Arcadia / Simon Chesterman.
Description: Singapore : Marshall Cavendish Editions, [2016]
Identifier(s): OCN 946560051 | ISBN 978-981-4751-50-6 (paperback)
Subject(s): LCSH: High school girls--Fiction. | England--Fiction. | Detective and mystery stories.
Classification: DDC 828.99343--dc23

Printed in Singapore by Markono Print Media Pte Ltd

"*Raising Arcadia* is a pacy mystery novel that has, at its centre, the irrepressible (and perhaps sociopathic) heroine Arcadia, a sixteen-year-old searching for her place in the adult world. Stuffed with intrigue and mystery, it will be adored by young adults and by adults who prize curiosity and challenge. Read it—and then read it again, to see if you noticed all the clues."

Adrian Tan, lawyer and author of *The Teenage Textbook*

"Chesterman's compelling creation of Arcadia, a preternaturally precocious sleuth with an unsettlingly clear-sighted and plain-spoken manner, is matched by the twists and turns of a devious plot, making for a true page-turner."

Philip Jeyaretnam, S.C., lawyer and author of *Abraham's Promise*

"In prose so still and measured, Chesterman methodically uncovers Arcadia's world. Beneath this astonishing portrait of a family is an invisible intellectual machinery at work that will intrigue readers at every turn. I am already impatient for the next book."

Leeya Mehta, author of *The Towers of Silence*

"What a mind-racing read! *Raising Arcadia* is *Fringe* meets *Perception*, Hermione meets Sherlock... a wonderful exploration of destiny *vs.* potential."

Sharon Au, actress and founder of styleXstyle.com

For M

CONTENTS

PROLOGUE

The knife is light in my hand. It is an extension of my hand. An extension of my will. Concealing it behind my back, I continue to smile and gesture with my right hand while the left prepares the blade.

They suspect nothing, of course. Their dulled senses do not perceive that even I struggle to keep my voice at its normal pitch, to prevent beads of sweat forming on my brow. All is outwardly calm, all normal. All illusion.

Amiably, I smile. I laugh. Yes, that is indeed an interesting story. All the while imagining it done. For it must be done.

And then I strike.

1
INTERVIEW

"Why do you think the other students don't like your daughter?"

The question dangles in the air like an accusation.

An uncomfortable silence.

"I mean, at home is her behaviour... normal? Does she play games, go to the park, and so on? Does she have friends?"

Brows furrow. Father looks to Mother, whose mouth opens and then closes again. Her eyes look to the ceiling and then to the walls, adorned with colourful project work. Uncertainly drawn maps; uneven charts of rainfall and sunshine.

"Because from what I can observe, she barely has any interaction with her peers at all." Gold-rimmed spectacles are pushed higher on the bridge of the nose, doubtless intended to underscore the seriousness of what is to follow: "If your daughter is to make anything of herself in this world, she is going to need to get along with people. She needs to learn to apply herself to the development of her character as well as the development of her mind."

A ruffling of papers in a disorganised file. The expectation that the parents would fill the silence is in vain. Mother is continuing to look about the room, as if searching for something.

"Have you at least addressed the question of her reading? She appears not to have the slightest inclination to adhere to the recommended list. You know, we spend months planning a suitable curriculum for the students to ensure that they are reading age-appropriate material that is of high quality and sound morals. Just last week I attended a conference on the very subject — in Majorca, would you believe. A rare perk for a teacher, I suppose." His tone has veered into the conversational, departing from the more serious timbre that he seeks. He straightens his tweed jacket, a cliché in need of dry-cleaning, and reverts sternly to type: "It is extremely disruptive to have one pupil refusing to read the books that we assign. And while her interest in anatomy is commendable, bringing first year medical textbooks to fifth form impresses no one."

Further consultation of notes. Reflected in the lens of the spectacles a few words that have been circled can be made out: "anti-social", "self-absorbed", "loner".

"Academically, she remains, shall we say, inconsistent?" Another page turns. "I mean, she isn't—what's the term we are supposed to use now—'intellectually disabled'. On those rare occasions when she does apply herself, she does tolerably well. In science, for example." This is a gross understatement. The teacher allows the parents a brief smile that is intended to be encouraging. Then his expression hardens once more. "But her disdain for subjects that she and she alone deems 'irrelevant' and her ignorance of basic facts about the solar system… Well, it was all I could do to prevent Headmaster from making her repeat the year."

Mother's eyes have almost completed their tour of the room, flitting past the puerile drawings of landscapes and self-portraits. They settle on a white sheet of paper fixed to the wall in a far corner of the room. With a light pencil and careful hand, a farmyard animal has been drawn. Or part thereof. The cross-section of a pig is easily identifiable, depicted with a level of detail that might be described—inaccurately—as loving. The animal is shown in profile, a vertical slice having removed the right half of its body from snout to tail. At first glance the image recalls a diagram of the various organs and humours hidden by fat and muscle, skin and hair. But on closer inspection it departs from such cool scientific models in its representation of a hog that has actually been cleft in two by some impossibly sharp blade, bodily fluids leeching down from the severed skin, guts just beginning to tip over the edge and fall down the page.

The teacher catches Mother's eye, apparently noticing the subject of attention: "And as for her sense of humour.

Well, no one was particularly amused and a few of the students had to see Nurse when she brought a frog for discussion time and proceeded to display its entire alimentary canal from mouth to intestine."

Looking down at his file once more, a tanned thumb and forefinger turn a well-worn wedding ring. A sigh, perhaps intended to seem sympathetic, escapes — or is released — from the teacher's wet lips. "I have seen many young men go through this school. They have gone on to the finest universities; many now occupy high office in government and in the City. Now that we have admitted girls as well I expect no less of them." His voice is earnest, apparently sincere. "It is our job to straighten the crooked timber of our youth so that they might make something of themselves. But we need your help."

Mother's hazel eyes remain on the sketched vivisection; her husband's turn from her to the teacher. Father nods and gives a slight smile that is taken as understanding.

"We had such hopes for your daughter," the teacher continues. "Your boy Marcus had done quite well here. Not so enthused about sports but — "

"Magnus," Mother corrects absently.

" — I'm sorry, *Magnus*. Your family really does have a penchant for odd names, does it not?" He allows himself a slight chuckle, but in the quiet of the empty classroom it is quickly extinguished by a corrective cough. Mother's eyes have returned to his and perhaps he thinks he has overstepped a line.

"Yes, Magnus was a remarkable boy. Exceedingly clever, but also obedient. I foresee an interesting future for that young man." The teacher appears to have confused obedience with Magnus's desire to pursue the path of least resistance. Clever, certainly — cleverer than she — but her brother's ambition stretches no further than the satisfaction of his appetites. He continues to breeze through university, concerned only to do well enough that he might be left alone. "Magnus shall land on his feet, of that I am sure," the teacher muses. "The question is: what are we to do with this one?"

Unusually, it is Father who speaks first. "Well, I suppose you could always expel her?"

Now it is the teacher's brow that furrows. "I don't think we are *quite* at that point. Though believe me the subject has come up in the teachers' lounge. I must tell you that there are those here who would be quite happy to see the back of her. But I was thinking more that we might work together on this." He leans forward and interlaces his fingers in a gesture intended to recall a church steeple, though it more closely resembles an ill-fitting set of gears. "If you might reinforce at home some of what we are trying to instil at school: discipline, honour — "

"Are you saying my daughter is undisciplined and dishonourable?" Mother has at last turned her full attention to the teacher, eyes narrowing ever so slightly as they do when she is irritated. Lips purse together and

a minute dilation of capillaries will soon lead to a flush of colour in her cheeks.

The teacher has not yet noticed this, but his weight shifts backwards, buttoning and then unbuttoning his tweed jacket as he moves: a sign of uncertainty. "What I am saying is that she needs more discipline and she needs a moral compass. The world owes no one a living. If she is to succeed in life she will need to be able to find the right path on her own. There is only so long that school, that *parents*"—a meaningful glance is unrequited—"can offer her structure. In the absence of that structure, some adolescents just… drift. They flit from one thing to another, never focused, never achieving their potential. For I do believe that your daughter has some potential." A magnanimous tone is now adopted, fingers tugging where a beard once grew in a gesture of staged thoughtfulness. An index finger rests a moment longer than it should on his now clean-shaven cheek. No sign of a blush there, but since vacation it has lacked its familiar red smudge. Stray whiskers on the chin suggest that this morning's shave was hasty. Curious.

"Potential to do what?"

Mother's polite sarcasm is missed by the teacher, who presses on with an enthusiasm that is only half-feigned. "Well, perhaps medicine? She has shown some aptitude in introductory biology. Her attention to detail in anatomy is, er, prodigious." A half-glance towards the half-pig in the corner. "And I gather you have something of a medical background yourself?"

Father clears his throat. "Well I suppose that's possible but at present she seems more interested in why things die rather than how one might keep them alive."

Mother smiles. "Yes dear, but the neighbours were so very pleased when she showed that those chickens had been killed by a fox and not their cat. Poor little beast would have been put down."

The teacher attempts to continue his thread of the conversation in the face of these distractions: "If she is to study medicine, she will need more than an interest in biology of course. General mathematics, chemistry. She will need to improve her overall grades considerably. In the event that she ever wants to practise medicine, the ability to relate to her patients as people will become essential. I'm sure you understand me, Doctor?"

Father shrugs. "She could always become a surgeon, so that her patients would be unconscious by the time they reach her."

"Yes. Well." The teacher tries to establish whether Father is joking. A slight upturn of Father's lips is taken as a license to let out another chuckle. "Oh I see you are having me on."

"What she really enjoys is puzzles," says Mother.

"That is well and good. I myself enjoy doing the crossword. But alas no one will pay me to do it. And I am afraid that your daughter has a tendency to look into puzzles that are quite frankly none of her business."

The brief diversion to career advice is over. More rifling

through pages of the thick file. The blue divider indicates the section devoted to disciplinary matters, which is quite thick. "The school remains grateful that your daughter identified the gardener who had stolen the German teacher's bicycle, but she must leave such matters to the proper authorities. And keep her prying eyes to herself."

For the first time there is a brief glare at the third chair, set back from the other two.

The teacher closes his eyes for a moment, collecting himself, before returning his attention to the parents seated before him. "The reason I invited you here this evening is that the start of a school term offers an opportunity to turn a page, to make a fresh start. It must not be a repeat of last term. I had hoped that a brief vacation would have allowed her to clear her mind, to mature. Yet her attitude continues to be one that I cannot describe as other than wilful insolence."

A pause to allow this to sink in.

"The final straw was that this morning she was found to have brought a prohibited substance onto the school grounds." A small plastic bag of coarsely cut dried leaves from the nightshade family is produced and held out silently for the parents to receive.

"Now that's not entirely her fault," Mother begins, nudging Father with her elbow.

Father looks down at the packet before slipping it into his own pocket. "That's right. I smoke a pipe now and then and she expressed an interest in the tobacco. She said she wouldn't smoke it, but wanted to compare it with the different leafs that she tells me some of the older boys and girls — and a few of the teachers — are known to smoke. I like to encourage her in her experiments."

In fact her taxonomy of tobacco is almost complete. Most of the smokers at the school consume branded cigarettes, notably Pall Mall and Lucky Strike, but there are a few who roll their own — in some cases lacing the shag with other herbs. Cigars and pipes are still less common.

"Would these be the same experiments that led her to amass a collection of dung so that she might examine the eating habits of the local fauna, and to hang a dead badger from a tree in the lower green in order to measure the rate of its decomposition?"

Father stifles a laugh and Mother slaps his knee in disapproval. But not very hard.

"As I said," the teacher is trying to regain control of the conversation, "a new term offers a chance at a new beginning. But she has to want to take that chance. She is now sixteen. Next year she enters sixth form and will begin her A-levels. The school aspires to help all our students succeed, but we cannot work miracles. Some of that drive must come from within. If she continues in this fashion, there is only so much that the school can do without compromising the education of her peers. I do hope you understand."

There is another pause and it is evident that the teacher has said his piece. The parents have not quite played their role, but he has done his duty to the school. Again, he waits to give them a chance to respond: to thank him, to reassure him of their support, to promise to discipline their daughter. But Father is simply nodding and Mother's gaze has returned to the pig.

The teacher looks from one to the other and then, for a second time, the third chair is the focus of attention. "Well, do you have anything to say for yourself?"

The finger on the cheek, the conference, the twirling wedding ring on well-tanned hands. Curious. There is little point debating the disciplinary matters raised. One could quibble about whether the rule against smoking properly applies to a student who brings pipe tobacco but no pipe, and there is no rule against dissecting frogs. Wilful insolence is a tautology—can one be insolent accidentally? But that is pedantry. The accusation of insolence assumes rudeness towards those deserving of respect. Do the teachers deserve respect? A more debatable proposition. By social convention, teachers are respected, perhaps, but that convention presumes that teachers have knowledge and wisdom to impart to their pupils. Another debatable point, present company particularly included. Explaining this, however, will incur the wrath of the teacher and perhaps upset Mother and Father. In any case, she keeps coming back to the cheek, the conference, and the ring.

It is only a second before the girl leans back and looks her teacher in the eye.

"You should buy your wife some flowers."

"I beg your pardon?" The teacher removes his spectacles as if they have somehow compromised his ability to see as well as to hear.

"I said you should buy your wife some flowers. Jewellery would be best, but at your salary you probably can't afford anything adequate."

"Young woman, you — "

"I say this," the voice slows, a concession that may be seen at patronising but she is beyond caring, "because she appears to be thinking of leaving you. Flowers are a customary token of affection, and sometimes serve as an acceptable form of penance for marital indiscretions."

Father clears his throat again, uncomfortably turning in the plastic moulded seat to catch his daughter's eye but it is too late.

"From the beginning of the year you typically arrived at school with a faint lipstick mark on your cheek. Some kind of upmarket brand, I'm guessing, from the matte finish and the fact that it remained visible for several hours. It's quite sweet, I suppose, the wife who gets made up prior to sending her husband off to work and gives him a goodbye peck. But one week ago the marks stopped appearing. Two possible explanations: either she stopped wearing makeup or she stopped kissing you. I'm assuming that your wife works — it's hardly likely that you could afford a car like yours on a teacher's salary — so she's still wearing makeup but not kissing you. That may be why you are now rushing to get ready in the morning and leave the house, evidenced by the patchy job of shaving today. Now one week ago was when you returned to school with something of a suntan, though you claimed to have been at a conference on educating today's youth. What kind of teacher feels compelled to explain to his students—and their parents—that he's been at a conference and that's where he got his tan? Someone who is trying very hard to stick to his story. Add to this the fact that just now when you were fiddling with your wedding ring one could see that the tan extends all the way under your ring. My limited experience in this area is that men tend to keep their wedding rings on in most situations, either due to fear of losing the ring or being accused of hiding the fact that they are married." The briefest of smiles at Father, who is now covering his face with his hands. "In any event, it is now clear that you spent last week in the sun without your wedding ring and are very keen to maintain your story that this was for a conference. No wedding ring plus lie equals affair. So, on the assumption that you are having an affair and your wife has found out about it, she is likely to leave you. Given that you depend on her financially, and taking into account any sentimental attachment you might have to her, you probably don't *want* her to leave you and so I suggest, once again, that you consider buying her some flowers."

The silence hangs once more.

"There's no need to thank me," the girl says. "Oh

and you might want to re-read your Kant because you're misquoting him. What Kant actually said was that out of the crooked timber of humanity no straight thing was ever made. Setting your goal as straightening all of us out puts you in direct opposition to one of the more influential philosophers of the second millennium. Though I suppose the fact that you're pitting yourself against a German may go down well with some of the school's more conservative alumni."

A tremor in the teacher's fingers and a clenching of his jaw muscles indicate an effort to remain in control of his temper. The gold-rimmed glasses return to the bridge of his nose. He clenches the pen so tightly that it is possible an act of violence is being considered, but then the fingers relax. It would be the end of his career and the start of a prison term to attack a student. "My dear young lady," he says at last, "your concern for my personal life is touching. But it is about the last thing that you should be worried about. What we are here to discuss this evening is your continuation at this school, the foundation of your education, and the prospects for a meaningful life. Does any of that register in your bizarre little head?"

The meeting is becoming tedious and Mother's shifting in her seat indicates that she would like to leave.

"It does," the girl lowers her head slightly in a pose of contrition. "I'm sorry that I've disappointed you." She looks from one parent to the other: "Mother, Father, I shall try harder."

The teacher is clearly unconvinced, but it is an opportunity to end the meeting on a more positive note. "That's better," he says. After a pause he closes his file. "You know, it is good that you have passions. But you need to bring some discipline to all your work and try to get along better with those around you. No one likes a smart aleck."

"Yes, Mr. Ormiston."

The teacher turns once more to the parents. "Do ensure that she reads the books on our list—and no more tobacco at school please?" He moves to stand up and the formal meeting is concluded. "I look forward to seeing you again soon," he says to the parents with a forced smile. "But not too soon, I hope!" He looks at the girl and is about to speak, but confines himself to a curt nod.

Hands are shaken and Mother, Father, and daughter step outside where the sun has set. They walk in silence along a paved path flanked by manicured lawns. Even in the lamplight, gentle indentations are still discernible where a student—the prints are too small and too light to have been a teacher—has ignored the "Keep off the grass" signs and taken a shortcut from the dormitory across to the woods that adjoin the school grounds.

They reach the car and climb inside. Father turns the key, but as they pull out onto a suburban street the girl asks for a favour.

He sniffs. "I'm not sure that tonight is the best time to be asking for latitude, my dear. It's late and we should get home."

She is loath to manipulate her parents, but does not want to let go — cannot let go — of the one interesting aspect of the evening. "I am sorry that you had to come in this evening, and I will try harder," she says. "But please do this for me?"

Mother turns to look at her for a moment. "Oh go on, Ignatius, humour the girl. Dinner can wait a few more minutes." Has Mother guessed what she is doing? No, but she knows something is afoot.

Father is not amused but also not in the mood for further argument. They follow the street until they reach a main road and the girl asks him to park opposite a row of shops. "Please turn off the lights — it's wasting battery power."

His daughter rarely displays an interest in conservation, but he simply asks: "And what are we waiting here for?"

"Just a couple of minutes."

He is nonplussed: "I mean *why* are we waiting here?"

The girl is peering out the window and does not reply.

Mother stifles a yawn. "I liked your drawing," she says. "It was quite lifelike. Well, deathlike. Ignatius, did you see her drawing?"

He did not but doesn't want to admit this. He is considering his response when a red sports car drives past them and parks on the opposite side of the street. A man emerges from the car, straightens his tweed jacket, and walks quickly past a fish and chip shop to the corner store, which doubles as a newsagent and a florist.

A minute passes before the man returns with a dozen roses. He pauses to adjust his gold-rimmed glasses and run his fingers through thinning brown hair, glancing only briefly in the direction of the car in which three figures sit in silence. Then he gets back into his own vehicle and drives off.

Inside the other car, the girl allows herself a smile of satisfaction. "OK," she says. "Now we can go home."

2
CODES

At dawn the next morning she, Arcadia Greentree, opens her eyes to regard the ceiling for a moment before swinging her legs down onto the carpet. Feet easily find a path between piles of magazines, books, and specimen jars to the bathroom. A stack of cosmetics samples — all unopened — balance precariously on the edge of a glass shelf. She moves a handful into the rubbish bin to restore the balance before sitting down. Nature's call answered, she quietly pads downstairs in a pair of fake Persian slippers, a dressing gown wrapped around her thin frame.

The house is silent. The last remnants of dinner have been cleared away, but the arrangement of the cushions suggests that Mother and Father sat on the couch to watch television after she retired to her room. A faint circle indicates that Father had one — no, two whiskies. A high probability that the programme was Mother's choice, then.

Later, perhaps while Mother bathed, Father went onto

the patio for a secret pipe. A black smudge on the railing shows where he cleaned up ash that spilled while tipping it into an ashtray. The ashtray itself has been washed and dried, but a slight residue of detergent suggests that it was he who washed it, and did so quickly in the hope of finishing before Mother concluded her ablutions.

As she moves towards the kitchen, an envelope stuck to the corkboard reserved for family notices catches her eye. Premium off-white bond paper. No stamp, no return address, the front merely displays a large "A" written in blue fountain pen. The flourish of the "A" indicates female penmanship even if she had not recognised Mother's handwriting. More interesting is that there are half-a-dozen unused thumbtacks in the cork. Others hold up postcards from Aunt Jean and Uncle Arthur's travels, a calendar from her school indicating holidays and a forthcoming concert, and a photograph of her elder brother Magnus. Rather than using one of the tacks loosely pressed into the cork on the left side of the board, whoever affixed the letter decided to do so with a steak knife — applying it with such vigour that the blade has pierced the cork and lodged in the plasterboard behind it.

She looks more closely at the handle, the angle of which is consistent with Mother's right-handed thrust. Small abrasions on the butt explain the force of its insertion: Mother removed a shoe with which to hammer it into the corkboard. All this was, presumably, to get her attention. It succeeds.

She eases the blade out, undamaged, and gives the knife a wipe before returning it to the cutlery drawer. The envelope she opens, peering inside before removing a single sheet of notepaper. The message has been typed on an old manual typewriter with a Courier font that now looks archaic. She examines it from different angles but it is the same bond paper as the envelope: reasonably high quality stationery though not particularly distinctive. The same bond paper in the same type of envelope as always—though the steak knife is new. The fingerprints on the envelope are probably Mother's, but unlikely to be part of the test. She dusted for them once, to be sure. Yet she did not find any prints on the note inside. Curious. On some occasions there has also been a faint rectangular-shaped residue on the envelope from some kind of adhesive, as there is on this occasion.

In any event, the first order of business is the words on the page. Eight sentences, seventeen lines:

```
Dear Arcadia, today's challenge will
exceed others. Real geniuses should
have no trouble with it. Code breaking
impresses no one: lies buried within
lies! In the end, the only thing that
anyone cares about is who won the war.
Second place is equal to last from the
standpoint of history. Column inches
shape that first draft of history as
```

```
we often see in great men and women's
rise and fall. Of course the days are
over when a trusted scribe could seek
to mould the way that your adventures
or reputation reached the public. This
highlights the way in which your every
deed lives on after your words and
especially punctuation. Message ends.
```

She studies the text, holding it up to the light as the message was once written in invisible ink. Not on this occasion. Lips move in silence, not reading words but proposing answers to questions that have not been asked. Code. Column. Ivory? A minute passes, lost in thought. She moves to the piano and opens the lid. A ten pound note and a sheet of lined paper, on which a short list has been written. It is only as she is picking them up that she notices another person entering the room.

"A full minute?" Mother asks, reaching the bottom of the steps. Although she is being playful, Arcadia has to suppress irritation at the implied criticism. "I thought thirty or forty seconds at most."

"Yes, well, piano keys haven't been made of ivory since well before I was born." She is sounding defensive.

"That's all right, dear." Mother plants an affectionate kiss on her forehead.

"But I do compliment you on the layered nature of this week's code," Arcadia smiles. "The use of the second column was a nice variation on an acrostic, but somewhat given away by the use of Courier font. A typeface with identical spacing that puts every letter in precise columns invites scrutiny for such a hidden message. In some ways it was redundant to point me to the second column with the message in the text itself. And as for the cipher text highlighting that one should pay particular attention to what comes after punctuation — well, I assume that step was more for symmetry than guidance."

"I thought you might appreciate it. A code within a code, within a code. Take each word after a punctuation mark and you get: 'Today's real code lies in the second column of this message.' And the second column of letters encourages you to 'Examine the ivories.' I thought it was quite neat."

"Well, technically it was a code hiding a cipher that revealed an obscure cultural reference." She is still irritated that Mother thought she had taken too long. "But yes, I concede that it was 'neat'." She glances at the notepaper, on which a short list is written — also in Mother's hand. "So, croissants, milk, fruit. Do we need anything for lunch?"

After breakfast she returns to her room and removes a violin from its case. She has told her parents that she must practise for Wednesday's concert, which is true, but she also plays the instrument to relax. As her bow moves across the strings, she loses herself in one of Mendelssohn's *Songs Without Words*—notes in their perfect order filling the room. Music is so much neater, so much cleaner than the world around her: it is possible to focus on one, just one thing, a pure note, and not the cacophony of reality.

As she plays she closes her eyes. Magnus once mocked her violin playing, back when she was screeching away on a quarter-sized fiddle laid across her knees. Over time she has improved considerably and is now preparing for her first solo performance in front of an audience at school. Naturally, Magnus soon found other qualities to deride, whether it was vocabulary or mathematical skills. Or there were games. In years gone by, her elder brother would occasionally summon up the energy to play chess in order to see in how few moves he could defeat her. Since the first time that she fought to a bitter stalemate, there has been no more chess.

On one occasion, only one, Magnus made fun of her appearance. It was soon after their final chess game and he had been eyeing the last cookie on a tray. Presumably to deter her from taking it, he had casually observed that she was becoming fat. She knew that many of her female classmates indulged in self-loathing over their weight, but also that her own was perfectly within the range of normality. At the time, she had simply smiled at him and eaten the cookie.

The only thing that does bother her about her appearance is her height. Having stopped growing at five feet, four inches, it is difficult to reach the highest shelves, where items of importance are often hidden. But she does not dwell on this. Her even-featured face, pretty enough, along with her long dark hair is of still less consequence. It has not brought her any admirers, which is a relief. In any case, boys who might contemplate flirting with her are generally frightened away the moment she opens her mouth. This is another thing on which she does not dwell.

Earlier that year, she had accompanied Mother to a shopping centre. Typically, she was left to roam the bookstore unless Mother needed her to help carry something. On this occasion, however, they were on the way back to their car when Mother realised that she needed some lipstick. So it was that they found themselves at the cosmetics counter purchasing a tube of Chanel's Gourmandise No. 76 lipstick. Mother tried to pay in cash and leave, but the nineteen-year-old sales assistant was sizing up her daughter as a potential customer.

"How about you, Miss? Can I interest you in something? Perhaps a little lipstick for you too? We have some lovely new colours that are just in."

Women and girls have been painting themselves in this way for several thousand years, so the chances of genuinely new colours seemed remote. The basic constraints are physiological: redness applied to the lips emphasises fertility and sexual availability. Any other colour—black, for example—strikes an uncanny note, and is therefore the colour favoured by goths in search of shock value.

"This is a lovely new Rouge Allure Velvet." The woman was still talking and offering her a chance to try out the lipstick— yes, the matte lipstick favoured by Mrs. Ormiston. She politely declined, while Mother waited for her change.

Many animals use colours to attract a mate, but more often it is the male that must do the attracting. Peacocks, for example, have brilliant iridescent plumage on their tails; peahens, by contrast, are fairly drab in appearance. How is it that the gender roles came to be reversed in humans? A subject for later study.

"Or how about some nail polish? I bet your friends would love this new lustrous blue flecked with gold."

Peer pressure? The sales assistant got points for perseverance if not for perception. Nail polish is more purely decorative and so the colour palette is wider. The Chinese, who may have invented it, favoured gold and silver until that became passé. The arc of fashion is long, but it bends toward repetition.

"What about lip gloss? We have some new glosses that are subtle and perfect for a first date."

This had become tiresome and Mother was worried that she might say something to make the sales assistant upset.

"Fine," she said reaching for a small bottle on the counter. "I'll take some sunscreen." Puzzled, the sales assistant added it to the bag, passed Mother her change, and turned to the next customer.

It is Mother who has convinced her to play in the concert, deploying her usual mix of flattery and filial obligation. It began with an overly-innocent observation about the concert at dinner, then a page from the school newsletter inviting interested students to put their names forward was strategically placed on her pillow. At last Mother asked her directly whether she would play. By that point she had already made the necessary arrangements at school and told Mother that she would play Mendelssohn. The moistening of her eyes clearly indicated happiness, but for a moment she was unsure whether Mother would laugh or cry. In the end she did both, hugging Arcadia. She has agreed to play because she knows how much pleasure it will give Mother, even though her music is primarily for herself. Mother does not ask much of her.

As she nears the end of the piece, her reverie is disturbed by a nagging sense that she has missed something, something important. Bow still moving, her mind ticks over the morning's events. Something about the code. Something different other than the knife.

For as long as she can remember, Saturday mornings have started with code-breaking, a challenge for her to solve in order to find a reward. At its earliest it might have been a sweet. In later years it had led her to a small present like a book or, as in this case, money and a shopping list for breakfast.

The codes or puzzles take many forms. The easiest were basic manipulation of a message, like reversing the letters in each word: "Raed Aidacra, yenom rof tsafkaerb si rednu eht enohp." Or simple substitution ciphers, like Caesar's code in which each letter in a message is replaced by a letter three steps along in the alphabet ("cat" becomes "fdw"), or numbers representing the place of each letter in the alphabet ("dog" becomes "4-15-7"). There have been a few variations using Morse code, and occasional use of the Freemason's cipher in which letters are drawn into a tic-tac-toe grid to generate geometric symbols.

Over the years, the puzzles have become more complex. But they always appear on the same off-white bond paper, almost always laser-printed in a simple font like Palatino. Almost always.

There is a knock on the door. "Is everything all right dear?" Mother asks.

"Yes," she replies, lowering the violin from her shoulder and moving to open the door. "Why?"

"You were playing the same note for five minutes. At first I thought you were doing an exercise, but I wanted to make sure you were OK."

She raises her eyebrows. "I must have drifted off."

Mother is about to go, when she calls her back.

"Yes, Arky?"

"Mother, we don't have a typewriter."

"No, dear." Mother looks at her, puzzled.

"Today's code was typed on an old-fashioned typewriter,

on which moulded letters on a typebar strike a ribbon. We don't have such a typewriter."

A fraction of a second. Mother's eyes break contact with hers and she reaches out to ruffle her hair. She says: "We borrowed the one in the office of one of your father's colleagues. His secretary still uses it sometimes to fill in forms. I thought you might find it interesting."

"Oh. All right then." She raises the violin back to her shoulder. "Sorry about the long note." As she returns to Mendelssohn, Mother's footsteps pause for a moment outside the room before she goes back downstairs. Mother knows that she prefers to play alone.

It is a long time since she can remember Mother lying to her. Innocuous lies concerning fairy tales and festivals ended at an early age. Around the age of six she nearly gave Father a heart attack when she laid a trap for the "tooth fairy". Admittedly, a mousetrap was a clumsy device with which to apprehend a dentally-obsessed pixie, but Father's fingers soon recovered.

The last occasion on which Mother lied concerned human reproduction. When she was nine, they had visited Aunt Jean and Uncle Arthur's cattle farm during breeding season. Having seen a bull and cow mating, she later asked Mother whether human sex was the same as sex for other species. Squirming slightly, perhaps from embarrassment, Mother replied that it was quite different. Making a child depended as much upon love as it did upon bodily functions, she said. Only with both could you create a

fully human child; it required more than the mechanics of insemination and gestation. Back then, Mother also broke eye contact and tried to distract her with a touch. Arcadia did not challenge her then, either, though she did some more research of her own on the Internet and concluded that human reproduction certainly looked a lot like the sexual behaviour of other mammals.

Dinner that evening is a simple meal of fish and chips as her parents have tickets to the theatre. "Are you sure you'll be all right, Arky?" Mother asks. "Ignatius, I'm not sure we should be leaving her alone."

"She'll be fine, Louisa," Father says, wiping his hands on a serviette. "She's more responsible than half the teenagers running around town these days. Aren't you, Arcadia?"

She reassures them both. "There hasn't been a burglary within a mile of our house in more than a year. And violent crime tends to be concentrated in the poorer neighbourhoods to the west. Please don't worry about me."

Mother is thinking twice about leaving her alone. "You can call our mobiles, and here's the number of the theatre in case they have one of those jamming devices." She passes her a piece of paper. "What will you do while we're out? Perhaps you could clean up your room? It's getting a bit dusty."

"I'll probably read. Perhaps conduct one or two experiments that I've been putting off." She sees Father's expression. "Don't worry, nothing explosive. I was thinking more along the lines of invisible ink." To reassure them and to encourage them to get on their way, she moves across to the stereo and puts on some Puccini. "You should probably start driving if you don't want to miss the opening."

Mother gives her a kiss, Father pats her on the shoulder, and they are gone.

She sits in a lounge chair, browsing through a reference work on spider bites until a quarter of an hour has passed. This allows enough time for her parents to realise they have forgotten something and turn back, or perhaps to circle around the block in order to check that she has not in fact blown up the house the moment they left her alone.

When there is no anxious knock on the door or jangling of keys, she stands and moves swiftly across to the writing desk by the telephone that her parents use to pay bills and write Christmas cards. A quick search confirms her suspicion that there is no bond paper in the drawers. There are stamps and envelopes, but simple brown ones for regular mail.

The envelopes with the codes appear only after she has been sleeping, so they could be anywhere in the two-storey house. But it is unlikely to be in a common area. They appear weekly, and so the stationery cannot be too hard to access. Almost certainly in the house, then, but not where she will stumble across it. Why? The paper is expensive but no more so than the drawing block paper that she requests for her anatomical sketches. She pictures the rooms of the house in her head, prioritising the search. For some reason her parents do not want her to find the stationery. It is presumably hidden somewhere they think she is unlikely to look.

Standing outside her parents' room, she realises that she is about to cross a line. The codes have been part of her weekly routine since at least the age of five. She had long assumed that Mother printed them on the family's computer—laser printing is so generic—but the use of a typewriter broke that mould. Was it a breach of trust comparable to that which she is now contemplating? Uncertain, yet it is clear that something is being hidden from her. And she needs to know.

She hesitates no more than a moment before opening the door. The room is neat—far neater than her own—with the simple furnishings of a queen-sized bed, a dresser, and a pair of reading chairs. From the wall opposite, doors open to an en suite and a built-in wardrobe.

Facing the bed is a painting of an English pastoral scene, which Father said depicted the estate that his family once managed. A small manor house sits amid rolling fields, a long driveway meandering up to the gates.

As she has seen Father do once before, she gently tugs at the bottom right of the painting and it swings out on well-oiled hinges to reveal a small wall safe with an electronic combination lock. Six digits are required to open the safe. A million possible combinations, and she has not seen Father enter the code. Trying one combination every second would take... two weeks. Or the safe may shut down after entering the wrong code. Yet she suspects that she will not need to resort to such brute methods. Six digits correspond to the abbreviated form of a birthday. She looks closely at the number pad: the zero is almost worn off, used far more than the other keys. The one and the six are also well-used. A quick review of birthdays in the family and she rebukes herself for not guessing immediately. She enters her own birthday into the safe, 6 January 2000: zero-six-zero-one-zero-zero. There is an ascending series of beeps, the internal locking mechanism slides across, and the safe swings open.

The chamber inside is about six inches high, a foot wide, and a foot deep. Careful not to disturb anything, she looks past the passports, a few bundles of cash, and some of Mother's jewellery. There are some old journals, or perhaps diaries, tied up with ribbons, but no stationery. She closes the safe and looks around the bedroom. It would have been too obvious to use the safe, and the noise of the locking mechanism is too loud. Mother would want the stationery somewhere to hand but accessible quietly. Something other than a combination lock that would protect it from prying eyes.

Underwear, perhaps? She opens the dresser drawer in which Mother keeps her brassieres and knickers. Though folded, it is clear that the undergarments have been hastily rearranged. She stacks them on top of the dresser in order to examine the base of the drawer. There is nothing else, but the drawer is too shallow. Feeling around the back, she identifies a small hole large enough for one finger to reach in and pull out the false panel. Behind it is a space as wide and high as the drawer but only a couple of inches deep, large enough to hold the carved wooden box that she now removes.

Placing it on the bed, she looks at it carefully. A Chinese style box, its deep red lacquer exterior is decorated in gold with a stylised image of a rabbit. It is large enough that it could comfortably conceal a reasonably-sized novel — or a stack of note paper and envelopes. Brass hinges on the back match a simple three-digit combination lock on the front. Only a thousand combinations this time, and from the design of the box it does not appear that an incorrect guess would cause it to become inoperable. Nevertheless, she pauses to consider the possibilities.

Three digits could be anything. A fragment of a phone number, a page in a book, part of a birthdate. She pauses. Dropping zeroes from her own birthday reduces to three numbers: six, one, zero. The brass lock does not move. She is contemplating testing individual codes when her eyes fall on the rabbit once more. As well as being a Capricorn in the Western zodiac, by the Chinese calendar, she was born in the Year of the Rabbit. Based on the lunar phases, the dates in the Chinese calendar are quite different from the Gregorian calendar used in European countries for the past half a millennium. A quick calculation would put her birthday as being on the thirtieth day of the eleventh month. Not reducible to three digits.

She turns the box over, looking for another way to open it, when a different possibility presents itself. In Chinese, dates are written in descending order year, month, day. Returning to the combination lock, she enters her abbreviated birthdate in reverse: zero, one, six. Even as the last number slides into place she hears a satisfying click as the notches align over the toothed pin inside. She slides a brass catch to the right and opens the box.

A stack of off-white envelopes — ten, to be precise — lie inside the box. Being sure to keep them in order, she lifts them out to confirm that all have been sealed. On the front of each is a yellow adhesive post-it note, indicating a date in the near future. The topmost envelope is marked for next Saturday, the second for the week after that, and so on. Up until the end of term.

She takes the envelope dated for the next weekend and examines it. The date on the post-it note is written in a hand she does not recognise. A man's, almost certainly, but as the dates are written using numerals only it is hard to get a sense of the natural handwriting style. The flap on the back has been sealed with its gum adhesive, activated by water or saliva. For a moment she imagines getting a DNA sample from the saliva, but this presumes access to a forensic laboratory. A more traditional method of investigation, then.

She takes the envelope downstairs and boils a shallow pot of water. When steam begins to rise, she holds the envelope over it, allowing the vapour to moisten the gum. In a few minutes, she can feel the gum loosening and turns down the gas. She eases the envelope open and eases out the paper inside.

Once again, it is something she has not seen before. At first blush, it appears to be a drawing rather than a message. A row of stick figures stretch across the page, apparently in the midst of some kind of dance. No, apparently at different stages of a dance:

Curious. Clearly another substitution cipher, but this time without a key. On the basis of frequency and position at the end of words it is highly likely that the basic stick figure with arms and legs outstretched like an X is the letter "e", but the sample is too small to extrapolate much beyond that. For meaningful analysis either several sentences would be needed, or else one would need the key.

Unless. The third word has seven letters, the first, fourth, and seventh of which are the same. A reasonable assumption is that it is "Arcadia". Letters from that word are repeated elsewhere in the message. Substituting them in produces a plausible result: "_ice__ d__e, Arcadia.

_ _ _ are _ear_ _ read_." Trying out the various remaining possible combinations, she arrives at the most likely final result. Curiously, it departs significantly from the usual codes that have directed her to a reward or a goal. On this occasion it merely congratulates her on approaching some goal that is as yet unclear:

Nicely done, Arcadia. You are nearly ready.

Odd. She waits for the envelope to dry before slipping the code back into it, resealing it, and replacing it in the Chinese box. She restores Mother's underwear drawer to its original condition and returns downstairs to continue reading about spider bites.

3
MISSING

"All right, if you can keep your distance please—there's really nothing to see here." A police officer is gamely trying to keep a curious public behind a line of yellow tape. "Police line: Do not cross", it reads. She turns to give Father a wave and lifts the yellow tape to enter the school grounds.

"Just where do you think you're going?" The police officer is new to the force, uncertainty being masked by bluster as he moves to intercept her path. His shoes are shiny and new; a barely concealed wince shows that they are causing him discomfort.

"Good morning, Constable." She looks him in the eye. "I'm a weekly boarder at the Priory School. My father has just dropped me off." The officer is hesitating. "As you can see, I'm too young to be a reporter, too small to be much of a threat, and I am wearing the school uniform. I think you can let me in."

The officer is taken aback but tries to hide it. He is still formulating a response when Mr. Ormiston appears. "Well, go on then, Miss Greentree, put your things in your room and get to assembly. You have——" a glance at the new watch on his wrist "——twelve minutes."

She nods at him and lifts her violin case from the ground, swinging her weekend duffel bag onto her shoulder. She is about to head towards the dormitory when she pauses. "Coconut oil," she says to the police officer.

"Excuse me, lass?"

"You could try coconut oil on your shoes. It will help them wear in faster."

The officer glances at her with suspicion, perhaps assuming that he is being made fun of. "I'll keep that in mind," he says at last.

"Well, Miss Greentree?" Mr. Ormiston begins.

"Yes, sir. Eleven minutes, sir."

"Exactly. Today of all days it would not be a good idea to be late." The teacher turns to the police officer. "Constable, that should be the last arrival of the morning. Please ensure in particular that the press do not intrude upon the school? We don't want this to become a media circus."

"Yes, sir."

Mr. Ormiston turns to see that she has not begun to walk across to the dormitories. "Can I help you with something, Miss Greentree?"

"No, sir," she says. A glance confirms the red smudge

on the teacher's cheek. She hoists the duffel bag once more and heads across to her rooms.

It was during breakfast with her parents earlier that morning when the telephone rang. Father had just passed her some more cosmetics samples that arrived in the morning post—Magnus's idea of a joke, she assumes. Mercifully, her parents have stopped suggesting that she open them.

Father frowned while listening, issuing a few questions before returning to the table. "Apparently there's a boy missing—one of the full boarders. They wanted us to know that there may be some police on the grounds today. The school hopes to keep the media out of it—but that seems unlikely."

"Who is the boy?" Mother asked.

"They didn't say."

Mother frowned. "And what does 'missing' mean?"

Father blew steam off his tea. "They didn't explain that either."

Arcadia took another bite of her toast, digesting the limited information. "They must be thinking it was a kidnapping. Bringing in the police so quickly means they think someone else was involved. Keeping the name out of the press might be intended to help with negotiations. But if that's the aim then perhaps they shouldn't have called the police in the first place."

"Well if there's been a kidnapping then you're not going near that school," Mother declared.

"Come now, Mother," she replied, "today is going to be about as safe as the school can get. Some of Britain's finest patrolling the grounds. You have nothing to worry about." She did not add that a repeat actor would be more consistent with a murderer than a kidnapper: the last time they discussed serial killers at breakfast had caused Mother to have palpitations. She kept the observation to herself.

It still took some time to persuade her parents that she could, in fact, go to school. In the course of the conversation, she variously promised not to speak to strangers, not to leave the school grounds, and not to put herself in danger. At last Father agreed to drop her off on the way to work — a little later than usual but probably acceptable in the circumstances.

Now, having deposited her duffel bag and violin in the dormitory, she walks along the paved path towards Hall. It crosses the grassy quadrangle, intersecting the path to the classrooms that she and her parents followed the previous Friday. The footprints that she saw that night are no longer visible, but a second, fresh set of prints that also cut diagonally across the grass can be seen — leading from a dishevelled climbing ivy at the base of the sandstone dormitory building.

She is about to look more closely when the first of nine bells rings, indicating that assembly is about to start. She quickens her pace as the second bell sounds, past the open door to Chapel, where Jesus stares down at the nave from his Crucifix. The third through fifth ring as she bolts up the stairs. She walks through the huge oaken doors to the sixth, and by the eighth has taken her place with her class, next to a pasty-faced boy only slightly taller than she but twice her girth.

"Just in time, Arcadia?" the boy beams at her, elbowing her painfully in the ribs. Sebastian, one of the least pleasant of her classmates, has a penchant for stating the obvious. She is about to reply when the ninth bell rings. At the front of Hall, Mr. Ormiston is standing before the lectern. At a nod from him, the school organist plays a few introductory bars, the students rise, and launch into a sombre rendition of "God Save the Queen".

God save our gracious Queen!
Long live our noble Queen...

The bobbing heads make identification tricky, but her own class is accounted for. Except for one mop of blond hair.

Send her victorious,
Happy and glorious...

She cranes her neck to look at the seats nearest the oak doors in case he arrived after she sat down. No.

Long to reign over us:
God save The Queen!

As the last line fades, Mr. Ormiston switches on the microphone at the lectern. A squeal of feedback causes a wince and a glare at the boys handling the audio at the back of the room. He quickly composes himself. "You may take your seats. Headmaster will now say a few words."

Mr. Ormiston steps back and the white-haired Headmaster rises from his ornate carved chair. Wearing a tailored suit, he is the picture of English respectability, down to a chin whose near absence suggests genetic connections to a noble line. He looks at the assembled group, scanning row by row as if to make eye contact with as many of his charges as possible.

"Ladies, gentlemen, it is a troubling day for the Priory School," he begins. "Earlier this morning we discovered an open window on the second floor of the dormitory building. A boy is missing."

Although the whispered news had already made its way through the serried ranks before the start of assembly, its confirmation by Headmaster still causes a gasp.

"At present we are cooperating with the police, who are looking into the matter. I want to assure each and every one of you that you are perfectly safe." Headmaster gives them a kindly smile, but it fades a little too quickly. "As a precaution, we have increased security, supplementing the private company that has long served the school with some of Her Majesty's Constabulary."

He brushes a stray lock of white hair back into place before continuing. "Many of you know Henry well" — so it is the blond mop of hair — "I myself spoke with him only last Friday. You may be worried about him. Please do not. The very best men and women in the land are working to find him and bring him back to us. I am optimistic that this will happen very soon. But if any of you have information that may help us, please let me or one of the other teachers know. We will be concluding assembly early, so if you have any information do come up and share it."

Another reassuring smile, turning to Mr. Ormiston who quickly echoes it. Headmaster continues: "This is a difficult time for all of us. But it is important that you all continue going about your business. So no tears, no fears. That is all."

Headmaster takes his seat and Mr. Ormiston goes over other, more mundane announcements concerning sports practices and the concert taking place on Wednesday. There is nothing further about the missing boy, Henry. But it is odd that they are asking for help from the students themselves. Clearly the school, and presumably the police, have very little to go on indeed.

When they are dismissed, a jabbing at her ribs reminds her that her tardiness getting to assembly left her sitting next to Sebastian.

"It's a shame," Sebastian is saying—he has adopted a tone of mock sorrow, but is clearly setting up some kind of joke. "It's a shame—that it wasn't *you* that got spirited away, eh Arcadia? Because you're kind of *arsking* for that, aren't you, *Arsey*? Eh? Am I right?" The pasty-faced boy looks around as if expecting applause. He has clearly spent much of the morning thinking this up.

"How I miss you on the weekends when I'm at home, Sebastian," she replies. She hesitates, as it is unlikely that the boy actually has any information. But it is possible that he knows more than what Headmaster has shared. "But tell me, Sebastian: do we know what happened to Henry?"

"Well," says Sebastian, savouring a rare occasion on which he may know more about something than another person. "Last night, around midnight, there was a creaking sound as Henry's window was opened from the outside. Someone silently sneaks into his room—ninja style—and then carries him off to who knows where."

"How do we know that it was opened from the outside?"

Sebastian rolls his eyes. "Well no one is going to break in from the *in*side, are they?"

She pauses, determining how to ask a question simple enough for Sebastian to understand without sounding so condescending that the boy is offended. "I mean, why do they think that he was kidnapped at all?"

Sebastian leans in towards her conspiratorially: "Because there was a ransom note. Left in his room, on his

desk. I hear it asked for a million pounds to get him back."

A ransom note written before a kidnapping has taken place? Possible, but against type. It appears that Sebastian knows nothing else and the lack of students heading down to see Mr. Ormiston or Headmaster suggests that there is not much more information to be had.

She reviews what she does know. Henry is in her class and a taciturn boy; built lightly as she herself is. His parents are wealthy but rarely come to the school. His father travels a great deal for work, Henry once said, though it is likely that this is not the only reason for the infrequent visits. During letter-writing periods Henry typically scribbles something cursory and then immerses himself in a book.

Though "friends" might be too strong a word, Henry and she have developed a nodding acquaintance based in part on their tendency to frequent little-used sections of the library. Henry has an abiding interest in fish of all kinds, which the library locates adjacent to its paltry collection of books on poisonous snakes and reptiles. The Dewey Decimal system has in this way led them to spend occasional hours in a quiet corner of the library, immersed in their respective passions and away from the noise of their peers.

Boys and girls are now beginning to stream noisily from Hall towards their classes. She joins the flow, peeling off at the quadrangle when she sees the young constable from the gate on the grass near the climbing ivy. Careful to avoid the footprints, she walks across to where the officer is adjusting the police tape that now cordons off the ivy and a few square yards of the adjacent grass.

"Good morning," she says to the constable, who looks at her suspiciously. "Need a hand?"

"No thank you," the policeman finishes with the tape and prepares to leave.

"It's just that I thought you would have wanted to cordon off a larger area. The footsteps continue in this direction for another ten yards."

A sigh. "Yes, lass, but they quickly reach the path and so are not much help. Here we have what we need: sufficient prints to get an estimate of height and weight and—and why am I even talking to you? The detectives will be here soon enough."

She nods in sympathy. Says nothing, but continues to nod and, as is human nature, after five such nods the officer feels compelled to say something more. "You've got nothing to worry about lass."

Kind, but not useful. "Thank you, Constable. But if you want I can give you an estimate of the height and weight."

"Really?" A patronising smile crosses the officer's face. "Do tell."

"Yes. I would say about five feet four inches and seven stone."

The officer frowns, mind ticking over. "That's a pretty small kidnapper."

"But within the normal distribution for a sixteen-year-old boy."

"I can see you don't know much about criminal investigation. Can you see this footprint here?" Next to the ivy is a clear print of a man's running shoe. "That's a size nine or ten shoe. Does your sixteen-year-old friend normally wear shoes that big?"

"It's a size ten and no he doesn't normally wear such shoes. They would be uncomfortably large and quite impractical for running. Nonetheless, it seems fairly clear that he made the prints himself."

The officer is still smiling, but uncertainty has crept into his voice. "Why do you say that?"

"Well, what's your theory at present? Kidnapper climbs up ivy, sneaks into room, drugs the boy, leaves a pre-written ransom note, carries the boy out the window, and then leaves a nice clear set of prints to find?"

Silence indicates that much of this is close to the mark.

"So let us review the flaws in this picture. First, it's a bold kidnapper who writes a note in advance of the actual kidnapping. If the kidnapping had to be aborted it would be evidence to be used against him. But I concede that it is possible. Secondly, however, look at the climbing ivy. There is no way that a man could climb down it carrying anything. In fact I doubt there is even a way in which a man could climb *up* it to the window. Given the current state of the ivy it's obvious that the primary damage to it was from someone climbing *down*. But thirdly, and most importantly, your key piece of circumstantial evidence has one major flaw."

"Oh, and what's that then?"

"The footsteps only lead away from the dormitory. Add to that the fact that they are clearly too shallow to have been made by a full-grown man, let alone a man carrying a sixteen-year-old boy—even a small one—and this looks less like a kidnapping and more like an escape."

"An escape? From what?"

She ponders this. "That I do not know. But the tracks go in the same direction as footsteps that I saw on this lawn on Friday night. Those were a little clearer and went from the dormitory across to the edge of the woods. I think that might have been a practice run for the real thing last night."

"So you're saying you think that this lad ran away?"

"It appears more likely than your kidnapping scenario. But if the story about the ransom note is true, then he went to some lengths to make it look like a kidnapping—including procuring a larger pair of shoes to make it appear that he had been taken." She sniffs in disapproval. "If Henry had been serious about this he should have made heavier tracks going to the dormitory and back, as well as propped up a ladder so that the carried-out-the-window theory could withstand some scrutiny."

"Yes, it's a shame that he didn't consult you first." The officer sees the logic in her deductions, but is perhaps unsettled by her suggestions as to how Henry might have improved the fake kidnapping. "So if he climbed out himself then where was he going?"

She pauses. "The tracks on Friday led into the woods. I'm assuming you have an alert out to look for him at nearby railway stations?" Again, silence indicates agreement. "So it would be risky for him to try to take public transport any great distance. But these woods go for a couple of miles before you get to the other side. There's a stream that would be difficult to cross at this time of year, though there are plenty of places to hide. If Friday was a proper rehearsal then he may have gone all the way to where he planned to conceal himself. Henry enjoys camping in general and fishing in particular. My guess is that he may be planning to stay in the woods for a little while as he contemplates what to do next."

She starts walking across the lawn towards the woods. When there are no accompanying footsteps behind her, she turns. "I promised my parents that I wouldn't leave the school grounds alone. Actually I promised them that I wouldn't leave the grounds at all, but I think that if I am accompanied by a police officer then they would understand. Come to think of it, I also promised them that I wouldn't talk to strangers — but again I think that a police officer constitutes an exception. So are you coming?"

She continues walking and smiles as a heavy sigh is followed by brisk footsteps that catch up with her as she reaches the edge of the woods. A well-trodden path leads in — little hope of finding usable prints there. But for a good half-mile there are no forks and the undergrowth on either side is undisturbed.

When they reach a point at which the path intersects with a wider trail, they stop. "OK, lass," the police officer says. "I think we should probably head back and share what you've told me with the detectives. They should be arriving any minute. I'm just here with a couple of the lads to protect the crime scene and keep the press out."

"Yes of course," she replies, but at the same time she is scanning the ground. Moving across the intersection she mentally divides the area into squares and checks each for prints or disturbances of any kind. Annoyingly, the wider trail is used by cyclists and the occasional horse. She is about to concede defeat when she at last spies a clear print in some damp ground on the continuation of the path beyond the intersection. She calls the constable over.

"That's nothing like the print at the bottom of the building," the officer says with frustration. "You're wasting my time—and I'm going to get it for leaving the school grounds."

"Look more closely," she says, pressing her own foot into the mud next to the footprint. "That's a size five men's hiking boot. Once he was clear of the school grounds he would have changed into his own shoes." She sees that the constable still doubts. "Officer, there are no other prints nearby. How many teenagers do you think have been out hiking alone in the past twelve hours?"

She sets off down the path. Another sigh, and once again the footsteps follow her further into the wood.

"This friend of yours. Why do you think he would run away?"

They have been walking for around twenty minutes now, the officer at last breaking the silence.

"I'm not sure," she replies truthfully. "Henry is a fairly quiet boy, no real enemies at school. The teachers are tough on him — but they're tough on everyone. He doesn't get along well with his parents, who are either in the process of getting divorced or should probably start thinking about it. Psychologically he appears stable enough — the rehearsal of his escape suggests that this was planned rather than spontaneous. Though it isn't clear what his next step would be after making it into the woods. His family is wealthy, but a teenager can only get so far travelling by himself before drawing attention. I should know."

The policeman lets this pass. "Does he have friends or relatives who live nearby? Anywhere he might be heading to?"

"Not that I know of. As I've told you, however, he is knowledgeable about camping and fish. My guess is that he's somewhere near the river, which shouldn't be too far from here."

The path bends and the trees begin to thin. They hear the river before they see it, the path winding towards a narrow point in its flow that causes turbulence in the water, a rushing sound that grows louder as they approach. Then the path ends abruptly at the water's edge, with a bench from which to admire the view.

"That's it?" The officer is getting frustrated again, doubtless fearing that he will be disciplined for having followed a teenage girl on a wild goose chase. "There's no bridge, no road?"

"As I said, given his interest in fishing and camping I think he's most likely staying somewhere near here. There is a rough trail that follows the river downstream and if you look carefully you will see another print from the same pair of boots. Not too far now, I think."

They set off down the smaller trail. It is only a few minutes before she stops and puts a finger to her lips, urging the police officer to quieten his clomping steps. She points off to the side of the trail, where a sheet of green tarpaulin has been hung over a rope lashed between two trees. Inside the simple shelter are a sleeping bag, a thermos, a flashlight, and a fishing rod. A small backpack has recently been used as a pillow. There is no sign of a boy, but a rustling in the trees too heavy to be a bird gives him away.

"You can come down now, Henry," she says without raising her head.

There is a pause, then more rustling, and a boy with matted blond hair clambers down from a nearby birch. He has not slept well and mud covers some of the freckles on his cheek. Interestingly, he appears both upset and relieved to have been found.

"I should have known it would be you," Henry says to her. He glances at the constable. "You didn't need to bring the fuzz."

She smiles to acknowledge the anachronism. "I'm afraid we were all getting a bit worried about you. The possibility of a kidnapping at the Priory School was just too exciting for some." It would be churlish to point out the flaws in Henry's plan, but she can't resist confirming her theory. "It was a nice touch, putting on the oversize shoes. Do you still have them with you?"

Henry grins despite himself. "Inside the backpack. I thought about dumping them, but if they were found then people would wonder what kind of kidnapper would suddenly decide to go barefoot."

"Listen, lad." The police officer is not trained for this, but adopts a kindly tone. "Why on earth would you want people to think that you had been kidnapped?"

Henry thinks for a moment. "I needed some time," he says at last. "I needed a break from— from everything."

"But your parents must have been frantic."

"'Frantic' is an exaggeration," Henry murmurs. "I don't suppose you know whom my dad called first: the police or his bank? It doesn't matter. I was hoping to have a couple of days of quiet, without..." his voice trails off.

"Is there something about your parents that you need to tell me, lad? Are you scared of them?"

A slight upturning of Henry's lip shows that this is far from the mark. But he is worried about something.

"What are you frightened of at school?" she asks.

Henry looks at her, eyes widening and then turning away. She mentally reviews the past week but there was nothing out of the ordinary. The brutish Sebastian operated within the school-determined boundaries for bullying—no physical contact that left a bruise or a cut. Classes were typical. As it was the last term of fifth form some of the students were anxious about exams, but Henry had always done fairly well. It was unlikely to be schoolwork. But it was something about school.

Something about Friday.

Headmaster.

She takes a step closer to him. "What happened on Friday?"

Now Henry's eyes open wide with alarm.

"What did Headmaster tell you? At assembly this morning he said that he had met with you on Friday. That evening you did your rehearsal of the escape, then spent the weekend gathering kit so that you could stay out here at least a few days. Am I right?"

"Of course, Arcadia," Henry whispers. "You're always right."

"So what could Headmaster have said to upset you so much?"

He looks down, unwilling or unable to answer. Curious.

She turns to the police officer who is standing awkwardly nearby. "Officer, would you give us a minute?"

The constable begins to say something then stops. He

walks a few paces away: "OK, but one minute only. And then we're all heading back to the school."

"Very well." She turns back to Henry and whispers: "Henry, what's going on?"

He looks up into her eyes and there is real fear there. Not the animal fear of a sudden and violent death, but the sustained fear of someone being forced to do something against their will. "I'm sorry, Arcadia. I really can't tell you."

"You really can, you know."

He shakes his head. "No, I can't."

She studies him. He is frightened, being forced to do something he does not want to do—and yet also cannot confide in another student about it. Not out of shame, but fear. Fear that if he were to share the information then worse things would follow. Is he acting to protect himself or someone else?

"All right, time to go back to school." The police officer has regained his composure and is keen to exert a little authority. "Let's pack all this up then and get moving."

They pack up the simple camp and return to the trail. Henry walks without enthusiasm.

"Whatever you are frightened of, I can help you," she tells him.

Henry smiles wanly. "Oh Arcadia, you can't even help yourself."

"Constable Lestrange, would you care to explain yourself?" A red-faced policeman — an inspector, from the epaulettes on his uniform — is growing redder from the exertion of yelling at the young officer as he emerges from the woods. "You are given the simple task of securing the crime scene until your superiors arrive. You then promptly disappear for more than an hour. I don't know what they are teaching in the academy these days, but the police force can only function if everyone plays their proper part. It is a team effort, Constable. Do you understand this?"

"Yes, sir," the officer replies, looking down at the ground.

"And do you recall what that device strapped to your body is for?"

Constable Lestrange half-turns to the handset on his shoulder. "Er, you mean my radio, sir?"

The red-faced inspector begins to turn an intense shade of purple. "Yes I mean your radio sir!" He takes a deep breath. "Now get back to the front gate and relieve Gregson. And why in God's name are you carrying a fishing rod?"

"Yes, sir. But first, sir, may I present Henry. The missing boy, sir."

The inspector takes a deep breath as if to resume yelling but catches himself. "The missing boy. Ah yes." He is weighing whether to congratulate or discipline the younger officer when a woman's cry cuts across the lawn.

"Henry!" An immaculately dressed woman is moving

quickly on high heels down the paved path. She pauses to remove her shoes before running across the grass to enfold Henry in an embrace. "We were so worried about you."

"We?" repeats Henry.

"Oh darling please don't be like that. Your father is terribly worried also. It doesn't matter. I'm so relieved that you're all right."

Mr. Ormiston is close behind Henry's mother. "There you are Mrs. Stamford. Safe and sound. Well done, officers."

"Oh yes," she smiles through moistened eyes. "Thank you so much."

The inspector's hue has returned to a ruddy pink. "Nothing more than our duty, Ma'am," he says without missing a beat. "I'm just pleased that Constable Lestrange and I were able to ensure young Henry was found and that all his, er, fishing tackle was properly accounted for." He is looking curiously at the equipment the trio are carrying, but smiles and does a half bow to Mrs. Stamford.

"In the circumstances," Mr. Ormiston says, stepping forward, "I think we can send you home with your mother. But we will need to have a little chat about what went on today. Soon."

Henry nods. His mother leads him back onto the path where she pauses to put her shoes back on.

The inspector eyes his subordinate officer. "Well, Constable. Don't you have anything you should be doing?"

"Yes, sir." He looks at the fishing rod still in his hand and passes it to Arcadia. "Thanks," he says under his breath.

"You're most welcome," she replies. "And thank you for trusting me. You know, Constable, I have a feeling we're going to be seeing more of each other." The officer is not sure how to take this and limits himself to a smile. He nods to the inspector and Mr. Ormiston and walks back towards to front gate.

Mr. Ormiston looks at her with suspicion. "And don't you have anything *you* should be doing?"

"I do, Mr. Ormiston." She crosses back to the path where Mrs. Stamford has finished putting on her shoes.

"Come now, Henry," his mother says. They also begin walking towards the front gate.

Henry turns back to her. "Thanks for looking for me," he says. "I just — " His gaze has drifted over her shoulder and he freezes, catching himself in mid-sentence. "Nothing," he says. "'Bye, Arcadia."

"Goodbye, Henry," she whispers.

On the walk towards the classroom block, she casts a surreptitious glance in the direction Henry was looking when he cut himself off. She cannot be sure, but from a window on the top floor of the administration block she thinks she catches a flash of white hair.

4
TROLLEYS

"What value is a human life?"

Mr. Ormiston paces across the front of the classroom, eyes roaming across the students at their wooden desks. It is the day after Henry's adventure and his customary seat by the window, adjacent to where she sits, is empty.

"And what would you do to save a life, or to save four?"

Mr. Ormiston enjoys periodically posing such moral dilemmas to the class. It is, presumably, part of his project to "build character" among his charges. Questions of this kind occur frequently in admissions interviews to university, of course, so there may be more base motives involved also—for the Priory School's high fees depend on its students getting into the best universities. Around a third will decamp in due course to Oxford or Cambridge, as Magnus did. Academic results are important, but so is one's presentation during an interview—particularly for those who lack a suitably noble pedigree or the kind of wealth that suggests naming opportunities for whichever college they attend.

"I want you to imagine a runaway trolley—a kind of single-carriage train."

Often the dilemmas are tedious: whether one may steal to provide for a starving family member; whether cruelty to animals is morally wrong. But sometimes the scenario to be played out is a little more interesting. The prospect of multiple deaths in a railway accident shifts her attention from Henry's empty seat back to the teacher, who has stopped pacing to draw a simple railway track running across the whiteboard.

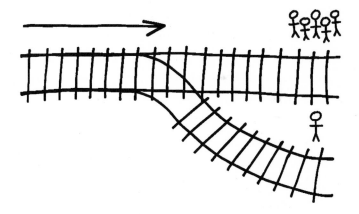

An arrow pointing to the right depicts the trolley. At the far end of the track, Mr. Ormiston adds five stick figures. Between the arrow and the stick figures, he creates a siding—and then adds a single stick figure to that.

"I want you to imagine that a runaway trolley is hurtling down this railway track towards a set of points. If nothing happens, the trolley will continue on the main line. Unfortunately, some villain has tied five people down to the tracks. There is no way to free them; no way to stop the trolley. If the trolley follows its current path all five will be killed."

He pauses for dramatic effect, suggesting once again that he had an amateur acting career at school—and perhaps university? No, the overacting suggests secondary school at most. He continues, raising an index finger for exaggerated emphasis: "But there is an alternative. You are standing by the tracks next to a lever that can divert the trolley onto a siding. If you pull the lever, the trolley will move onto that track and the five will be saved. Alas, that track passes through a narrow gorge in which a deaf workman is doing some repairs. There is no way to warn him or stop the trolley. So if you do divert it, he will certainly be killed."

Mr. Ormiston stops pacing, enjoying another theatrical moment. "So the question is: do you pull the lever or not?"

Interesting, but surely the wrong question. Tied to a track by whom?

"Why can't you stop the trolley, sir?" The oafish Sebastian has put up his hand and Mr. Ormiston has nodded for him to ask his question.

A sigh. Because that's how the problem was defined, of course. But the teacher makes the mistake of elaborating.

"Let us assume that the brakes have failed. Eventually the trolley will stop due to friction, but not until well after either one man or five have met their grisly end."

She raises her own hand. Another sigh. "Yes, Miss Greentree?"

"Where is this taking place, sir?"

"Does it matter?"

"Well, depending on the type of points it may be possible to pull the lever while the trolley is crossing the junction. This would send the front axle down one line and the rear axle down the other, derailing the trolley and saving all the people. If it's a tongue and plain mate switch, historically used in parts of the United States, then —"

Mr. Ormiston is becoming irritated. "No, it is not possible to derail the trolley by moving the switch back and forth. It's a *hypothetical* point switch. Indeed, that's the 'point'." His irritation dissipates as he laughs at his own little joke. He coughs and continues: "Nor can you pile up rocks on the track or in any other way stop the trolley. The question is whether you do nothing and allow five people to die, or pull the switch — saving them, but condemning an innocent man to that fate."

Innocent is of course the key point here. But the teacher is keen to get on with his hypothetical, prelude to some hypothesis about the conflicting nature of moral obligations that he wishes to keep up his sleeve.

"And so I will ask you to reflect for a moment and then vote. Would you pull the lever or not? You must do one or the other — failing to answer means that you are allowing five people to die. So which will it be? Those who would pull the lever, raise your hands."

The shuffling of sleeves being raised indicates that virtually all the students would pull the lever. Mr. Ormiston looks keenly around the room. "Very interesting. Yes, that is consistent with a majority of people's responses. It reflects a basic human desire to minimise suffering and maximise happiness: what the philosophers call 'utilitarianism'. I think we can assume that the five you save would be happier than if they were dead."

He pivots on one foot. The brief secondary school acting career appears to have included a musical. "But not all of you chose to pull the lever. Two of you would have let five people die, rather than one. Why?"

She prepares to respond, but Mr. Ormiston is addressing someone at the back of the room. None of the boys who sit in the back row has said anything remotely interesting for the entire year, but the teacher's gaze is too high. Either one of them has stood up or someone else has entered.

"Because it's not right." Henry has just walked in, having heard enough of the scenario to take a position. "It's wrong to kill — even if you think you're serving some larger good. You don't have the right to decide that some deaf workman should die."

"Good, good," Mr. Ormiston nods for him to take his seat next to her. "Most people would pull the lever. That's the utilitarian in us. But I hope that even those who took such a decision felt at least a twinge of guilt. What Master Stamford is showing is that a number of people feel that doing the right thing is more important than simply looking at the consequences of one's actions. In short, one should do the right thing because it is *right*, rather than because it leads to a particular outcome. The philosophers call this 'deontology' or duty-based ethics."

He writes "utilitarianism" and "deontology" on the board. "This 'trolley' dilemma is a useful one because it highlights the tension between a moral framework based on consequences, and a morality based on rules." He looks at her, "And you are our other deontologist, Miss Greentree? I confess I wouldn't have taken you for a rules-based philosopher."

"Not quite," she replies.

"Yet you wouldn't have pulled the lever."

"No."

"Not even to save four lives."

"Not even to save *five* lives. But a person doesn't get tied to a railway track for no reason. We may not know much about this group, but it is highly probable that their involvement is not accidental. They are being murdered. This is, therefore, a crime scene. If we interfere in the murderer's scheme he or she—statistically, we can say 'he'—will know that he is under suspicion and go to ground. By allowing it to proceed he may make a mistake and thus be caught. One could argue, I suppose, that saving the lives of the five bound victims would make it

possible to interview them and identify the likely murderer that way, but forensic evidence around the bodies would probably be sufficient — despite the inevitable mess caused by the passage of the trolley."

Mr. Ormiston has stopped pacing and pivoting, his mouth slightly open. A pause as he takes a deep breath. Rather than answer, he turns back to the board, erases the siding, and adds a bridge with another figure standing on top of it. Unlike the anorexic stick figures, this new figure appears to be morbidly obese.

"Let's try a different but related problem," he says. "Imagine the same scenario, though instead of a lever operating a set of points you find yourself standing on a bridge under which the trolley is about to pass on its way to the five victims. You know for a fact that a heavy weight dropped in front of the trolley would stop it. As it happens, on the bridge next to you stands a fat man of precisely that weight — and he is leaning against a weak handrail to watch the progress of the trolley."

Again a moment's silence in a bid to elevate the drama, before the dilemma is presented with a flourish: "Would you push him over the edge?"

Some of the students are tittering now. One of the boys makes the mistake of whispering a little too loudly that the fat man looks like a certain member of the class and gets a whack on the back of the head from Sebastian.

"Master Harker, that is enough," Mr. Ormiston intones — though with no intent to punish him.

"Now before you ask, let me tell you that you cannot jump heroically onto the trolley and stop it yourself. Nor can you sacrifice yourself and stop the trolley, because you lack the requisite mass. Your only choice is to push the fat man or allow the trolley to continue on its path. So I ask again," he says, "would you push the fat man over the edge to stop the trolley and save the five victims? Raise your hand if you would."

A single hand. A further sigh. "Yes, Miss Greentree?"

"I'm inferring from your earlier response that the innocence of the five victims was to be assumed. In that case, and if we are primarily trying to reduce the number of casualties, and if there is no additional information about this rotund trainspotter, then pushing him over the edge is no different to pulling the lever that diverts the trolley and kills your deaf workman."

Mr. Ormiston forces a smile. "Thank you, Miss Greentree." He turns to the rest of the class. "For *most* people, the idea of physically pushing another human being into harm's way is different from pulling a lever. We tend to view it not through the cold lens of utilitarianism — even though the numbers are indeed

the same, five lives versus one. Instead, most people see the injunction not to kill as being paramount when faced with a flesh-and-blood person."

Another suspicious glance at her. "My point is that how we frame these questions can sometimes determine how we answer them. Let me illustrate this by a final example — building on Miss Greentree's desire to find the villain who tied the five victims to the railway track in the first place. So now let us assume we know that the fat man is, in fact, the villain. The trolley, once again, is hurtling along towards the five helpless individuals. Who would push this fat villain into the path of his own instrument of murder?"

All the hands go up. All except one. The teacher is considering pretending not to see her, but she politely clears her throat.

"Yes, Miss Greentree? Everyone would happily give this miscreant his just desserts. Why are you suddenly so merciful?"

Her eyes move from the teacher to the round figure on the whiteboard, standing on the edge of the bridge. "Because if we push him in front of the trolley, we may stop his crime — but we would never know why he did it."

The school bell rings to signal the end of the class, barely covering Mr. Ormiston's whispered "Thank God," before he ushers the students out.

"Well?"

As the class moves through the cloisters towards the school gymnasium, she matches step with Henry.

"Well what?" Henry looks straight ahead, again doing a bad job of hiding something.

"Well, what were you running away from? What did Headmaster say to you on Friday?"

Henry quickens his step to move away. "Not here, not now. You know that the walls have ears, Arcadia."

She allows him to leave. Not only ears but eyes, of course. A glance and a smile at the black hemisphere fixed in the ceiling of the corridor. Behind the darkened glass is a camera, silently observing its surroundings. Most of the classrooms and thoroughfares have them. After the weekend's excitement their coverage will almost certainly be extended further across the open areas of the Priory School.

The school has been her home during weekdays since she started as a yearling at the age of thirteen. She was taught the idiosyncratic argot of her English public school the day she arrived: first year students were referred to as "yearlings", second year was called "remove", third year was in fact "fifth form", while the sixth form actually took up years four and five and completed secondary school with the taking of A-levels.

Established by the Church of England almost two centuries ago, the Priory School was until recently one of only four English public schools that remained boys-only and boarding-only. Three years ago, she was part

of the first intake of girls to join the school—a decision that remains a point of controversy with some of the older alumni.

Today five hundred students live on campus, most of them for the entire school term. Only a few whose parents live in the vicinity are allowed to board on a weekly basis, as she does. The majority of the students are still male and some of the traditions—and not a few of the teachers—are taking time to adapt to the presence of women on campus who are not there to cook or clean.

The Priory School's motto is "*Ipsa scientia potestas est*"—knowledge itself is power—yet it can hardly be described as rigorously academic. The Board somehow obtained an exemption for its students to go straight on to A-levels without completing the earlier GCSE exams, but this seems more testimony to influence than intellect. The guiding principle appears to be that the world is to be run by well-rounded young men who play rugby in winter and cricket in summer and know their way around a church service.

The teachers are well-intentioned enough. Mr. Ormiston, form teacher for this, her fifth form year, can be tiresome but is genuinely keen to get the most out of his class. He is strict—imposing a discipline clearly inflicted on him as a young man at his own boarding school—but does not take undue pleasure in the discomfort of his charges.

Some of the other teachers, by contrast, exhibit tendencies towards sadism that have been expunged by most of the world outside the English public school system. Caning is technically forbidden — indeed, it has been illegal in England for almost two decades — but in practice is still used by a small number of teachers. More than once, she has seen the science teacher, Mr. Pratt, flushed and with beads of perspiration surely not occasioned by the physical exertion of whacking a teenager with a light piece of rattan.

She herself has been the recipient of such discipline on only one occasion. In an exceptionally tedious science class, the aptly named Mr. Pratt was going on and on about the solar system and so she took out a crime novel to keep her mind occupied. The science teacher took this as some kind of personal insult and stopped next to her desk.

"Miss Greentree, would you do us the honour of recalling the names of the planets?"

She put down the novel. "Five Roman gods and one goddess, a Greek god, and the Germanic word for 'dirt'. Or something like that."

Mr. Pratt clapped twice, slowly. "Very funny, Miss Greentree — though as you can see I am not laughing. I am aware of your disinterest in this field, but unfortunately you do not set the science curriculum."

"I'm not disinterested, sir, I am *un*interested. Disinterest would suggest that I am impartial or fair-minded about the matter. *Un*interested makes it clear that I do not care to know more about it."

Any unhappiness about the criticism of his word choice

was overshadowed by incredulity at the sentiment. "But this is the physical universe — it is our very existence."

"Perhaps. But the brain has a limited capacity for storing information and I fail to see how any of this is relevant. In our lifetime it is inconceivable that anyone will do more than scrape the surface of any of these planets. Their movement will have no more impact on me than the horoscope that you read over lunch sitting by yourself in the staff lounge will have on your own life. So I prefer to keep space for subjects that are more likely to be of some practical application."

She sensed the teacher's rising blood pressure, but could not resist adding: "I for one intend to forget all of this as soon as the class is finished."

"Well let's see if we can't help you remember it," Mr. Pratt said, licking his lips. "Five strokes of the cane, Miss Greentree. For insolence."

She moved to the front of the class as he took out the cane. "Hold out your hands, please," he said.

"If it's all the same to you, I'd like to be punished in the same way as the boys. Women's liberation and all that, you know."

His eyes narrowed and he pursed his lips. "Very well."

The pain of the beating was intense but transitory. Having seen the routine before, she stood facing the board in front of the class, determined not to make a sound. She slowed her breathing and relaxed her body, allowing the blows from the rattan to sway her gently like a sapling. The absence of a reaction seemed to further rile her teacher, as there was an escalation in the force of the third and fourth hits — apparent even through the numbed flesh of her buttocks. The cardboard that she had placed in her rear pockets prior to the class as a precaution absorbed much of the impact, but she was still going to have bruising there tomorrow. The odour of Mr. Pratt's sweat mixed with stale cigarette smoke — Lucky Strike? — wafted across her. She could hear the teacher's breathing deepen as he raised the cane above his left shoulder for a final strike.

"Is everything under control, Mr. Pratt?" A quiet but authoritative voice from the doorway.

The distraction caused the teacher to slow his swing and the last blow was by far the lightest. Mr. Pratt turned to face the white-haired gentleman at the door, who gave a good impression of having popped in on his way somewhere else — though the classroom was the last door at the end of a hallway, and therefore not on the way to any other part of the school.

"Yes, of course, Headmaster," Mr. Pratt replied, trying to get his own breathing back under control.

"Very good, Mr. Pratt." Headmaster nodded to her: "Good afternoon, Miss Greentree." The door closed and he was gone.

That is one of the few times that she has seen Headmaster outside assembly. Though he has run the Priory School for as long as she has been attending, Headmaster remains a presence more felt than observed.

Even now, as at today's assembly, his interactions with the students are limited to the formal — welcomes to students and parents, set speeches at school events, and missives sent through the school newsletter. He teaches no classes and holds no office hours.

Over the years, she has amassed basic information about his background. Despite the lack of a chin, he is not of particularly noble birth. He grew up in and around London, his father having some position of significance in a newspaper — retiring before that industry's death spiral began. An Oxford education led to two decades teaching at the nearby public school Radley College. An unusual move, it might be thought, for someone who once showed promise in scientific research. But it sowed the seeds for a career in secondary school education. In that sense, Radley was a good choice as it had a prominent name and good connections.

In time, he appeared to gravitate towards administration and fundraising, rising to the position of Sub-Warden at Radley. After a few years as number two, he applied to the Priory School and was appointed Headmaster by the school board about a year before Magnus first enrolled.

In the ensuing decade, he sought to insulate the school from the obsessive testing that has come to dominate much of education elsewhere in the country. On its face, the Priory School aspires to cultivate confidence and positive values in its boys. This is reinforced through sport and culture. The decision to extend that education to girls had been justified in part by the expansion of opportunities for women, but also because their inclusion would offer a more diverse environment the better to foster the moral development of its men.

Yet beneath the façade of holistic education lies an elaborate system of monitoring. It is subtle, to be sure, but just as the black hemispheres hide cameras and microphones, the absence of tests does not mean the lack of assessment.

The file that Mr. Ormiston produced last Friday, when her parents were called in, is one example. The full extent of that monitoring is unclear, but it is a safe assumption that extensive data is kept on all the students. Odd, then, that something like Henry's disappearance could not have been predicted.

None of this, in any case, has diminished the Priory School's attractiveness to the great and the good. Though not mentioned in the school's promotional literature, the fact that various members of the British Royal Family once slept in its dormitories is partial explanation for the length of its waiting list.

Within the school, there continues to be speculation as to which beds were previously occupied by two of the current heirs to the throne. Based on proximity to fire escapes and evidence of subsequent renovations to remove doors to adjoining facilities for bodyguards, the answer appears fairly clear: rooms on the second and third floor of the dormitory building, respectively.

Given such august company, it was sheer chance that Magnus was admitted. Their parents had neither the connections nor the money that were tickets of entry for most of the boys at that time. Instead it was an accidental encounter when Headmaster himself went to Father's clinic for a routine check-up. The fact that a boy had withdrawn close to the start of term came up in polite conversation and Father mentioned that his eldest son, Magnus, was about to start at a state-funded comprehensive school. A few days and telephone calls later, Magnus was called in for an interview; soon afterwards he was offered a full scholarship. Seven years later, the school had announced that it would take in its first cohort of girls and she followed in Magnus's footsteps — though, as the latter never tires of mentioning, the younger Greentree received only a half-scholarship.

Her interview for admission to the Priory School remains the longest conversation she has had with Headmaster. Even then his luxurious mane of hair was completely white, trimmed as always just above the collar of his customary dark suit.

At a little over six feet, Headmaster was a physically imposing presence. But what struck her most on that first occasion was that he spoke to her as he would to an adult. There were no games, no pretences — though in retrospect that was, presumably, precisely the game he was playing. At the time it was refreshing.

"Why are you here?" Headmaster said, barely looking up from his papers as she and her parents were ushered into his office overlooking the grassy quadrangle. He sat at a large oak desk, his back to the window. The desk was empty except for a lamp, a stack of papers, a golden letter opener that resembled a small sword, and a black cloth that had been draped over three small boxes.

It was immediately clear who should respond. "I would like to come to your school."

"Why?" He signed two documents with the fountain pen, an indulgent swirl of a signature with his left hand as his right moved the papers into a drawer, and opened another file.

She paused. "You have a laboratory. My brother told me that science classes actually do experiments. Most of the other schools just use books in science. Your library is also better than many schools — though not as good, obviously, as the British Library in London."

"Obviously." Still pretending to attend to his files.

"And the teachers here are better educated and, by the look of the cars in your parking lot, better paid than the average."

A flicker of the lip, almost a smile. Headmaster now looked up at her: "Not *that* well paid. But tell me: why should I let you into our school? This school produces leaders of men: generals, prime ministers. Kings. What makes you think you belong here?"

"Not all of your boys become generals or prime ministers. And the ones who become kings don't have much say in the matter. You need the occasional student like me here so that the others can say that they met someone whose parents had a trade." This was not a kind way to describe Father's medical career, but from what Magnus had told her it was an honest description of the school's demographics. "And now that you've decided to admit girls, you want to ensure that the first batch aren't so dim that they bring down your ranking in the league tables."

This earned her another twitch of Headmaster's lip. "But I forget myself. Do please sit down." He pointed vaguely to the single seat on the other side of his desk. She sat. Mother and Father looked about, then settled into a pair of chairs by the door of the office.

"Here at the Priory School we don't believe in standardised testing. Instead we seek to draw out the very best in each boy — and girl — helping them achieve their potential. I believe that every child is like a candle: our job is to provide the spark and see how brightly he or she can shine. For today, I have only one question that I would like to put to you, to see how your mind works. That will help me determine whether you are right for our school, and whether we are right for you. Are you ready?"

The preliminary question was rhetorical.

Headmaster lifted up the black cloth on his desk, revealing three cubes, each about two inches wide, deep, and high. One was painted red, one yellow, the other blue. Apart from the colour there was nothing to distinguish them. Wooden, made by hand, painted several coats with a thick brush, they were probably made for this game.

"What is underneath them?" she asked.

"Good, you are observant. Yes, these are hollow cubes with the open side face down on the desk. If I tell you that under one of them is a boiled sweet, which one would you pick? Choose it, but please do not touch it."

An unusual test. Not looking for colour-blindness or one cube would be green. Boys her age tended to like the colour red: did the school desire conformity or individuality? But clearly something more was going on here. This was not the test. That would come later. Hence it did not particularly matter what she chose.

"Yellow," she said without hesitation.

"Very well," Headmaster said. He reached over and lifted the blue cube carefully, showing her that it was empty and setting it to one side. "So we know now that there was nothing under the blue cube. And here is the question on which much will depend: If I tell you that the boiled sweet is in fact under one of the remaining two cubes, will you change your selection? You have chosen yellow. Would you now like to change to red?"

A game of chance, but something more than that. She ran through the combinations in her head—red, yellow, blue. An interesting problem in theory, but to do it in practice required more than luck. It required skill.

"No thank you, I am happy with my choice."

A slight contraction of the eyebrows: Headmaster was disappointed. "That's a common response, but I confess that I expected more from you. Though the mathematics is clearly beyond the normal thirteen-year-old, I thought you might have worked it out intuitively.

"Let me explain. There are three cubes and three possibilities: the sweet could be under the red, or the yellow, or the blue cube. So you had a one in three chance of choosing the right cube at the start. You chose the yellow cube, and so there is a one in three chance you were correct. In that case, switching cubes would be a mistake. But if the sweet was in fact under the red cube, you were wrong. I have now taken away the blue cube, however. If you switch to the remaining cube, then you would have won. Similarly, if the sweet was under the blue cube, you were wrong again—but in that case I would have to remove the *red* cube, and you would win again by switching. So in two of the possible three scenarios, you are better off switching from your original choice.

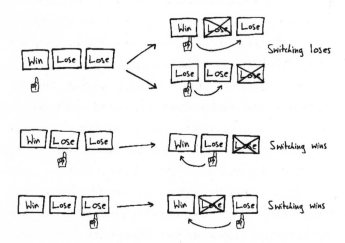

"I can make it clearer. Imagine that there are not three but three hundred cubes. You choose one, I then remove two hundred and ninety-eight other cubes, leaving the one you chose and one other. The sweet is under one of the two cubes. Would you really not switch?"

Throughout this, she had kept her eyes on the red and yellow cubes. "I thank you for the explanation," she said. "But my task was to determine under which cube the boiled sweet is *in fact* to be found. I chose the yellow cube, but as it happens I am not especially partial to boiled sweets. Mother says they are bad for my teeth. We can still solve this puzzle, however, if I lift up the other cube." She swiftly reached over and lifted up the red cube, which was also empty.

"As the sweet is not under the red or blue cube, we can deduce that it must be under the yellow cube." She left the yellow cube untouched, however, in the centre of Headmaster's desk.

The bark of laughter was so unexpected that it startled her. Headmaster's white hair shivered with mirth to the point that he wiped his eyes with a pocket handkerchief. "Oh, you will do well here, my girl," he said, continuing to chuckle. "Report to school at 8am on the first Wednesday of September. That is all."

It was clear that the interview was over. She stood up and urged Mother and Father to do the same. Headmaster shook her parents' hands warmly and wished them well, ushering them towards the door. They were confused, but

as the outcome was positive did not see a reason to protest at the speed of the interview.

At the entrance to his office, Headmaster was about to close the door but called out to her. "Miss Greentree, if your mother makes an exception, you may enjoy this — it's blackcurrant, I believe. You've earned it."

She caught the purple sweet and nodded to Headmaster. Up his sleeve, most likely. "Thank you, sir."

On the desk, the yellow cube remained in its place.

Once they reach the gymnasium, the students go to the boys and girls lockers to change for physical education. The school's facilities in this area are extensive, including a cricket ground, rugby field, swimming pool, and a nine-hole golf course. Over the years she has developed an interest in the sport of fencing, and is beginning to learn boxing — thus far confined to practice with a punching bag. During class, however, the focus tends to be on team sports and today they will be starting with a round of mixed Eton Fives.

The Priory School is one of few that have regulation courts for this uniquely public school game. Though played by hand, the court and rules are similar to squash. The aim is to prevent the ball bouncing twice before it is hit up against a wall. This can be done using any combination of the side walls or a small ledge that runs around the court.

The court is modelled on a chapel at Eton College, where the game was first played almost 150 years ago. Among the oddities of the court are a step in the middle that divides the front half from the back and a projection from the left wall known as a buttress. These obstacles complicate movement around the court and routinely interrupt the flight of the ball. The point at which the buttress meets the step is known as the "dead-man's hole". In the original chapel, this was some kind of drainage point, but in modern courts it has become a small niche from which it is almost impossible to return the ball.

Fives is now played as a doubles game, with the team that gets to twelve points first winning. The ten boys and six girls in her class have been divided into pairs, mostly mixed. She is partnered with Henry, and a glance at the chalkboard shows that their first — and probably last — match is against Sebastian and a thuggish girl by the name of Joan Hardy who, it appears, made it into the school based more on her ability to row than to think.

Points in Fives can only be won after a team has served the ball. In many other ballgames serving provides an advantage, but Fives allows the receiver, known as the "cutter", to reject serves that are too hard to hit.

As she and Henry put on their white gloves, she regards their opposition. Both Sebastian and Joan are at least a stone heavier each, with correspondingly greater strength. They will rely on power; she and Henry must rely on agility. A whispered discussion leads to a basic strategy of hitting the ball towards the buttress that juts out from the wall. If it connects, the ball will bounce back towards the front wall and be very hard to hit. If it misses, the ball will still be on the left hand side of their right-handed opponents.

Predictably, Sebastian and Joan hit the ball as hard as they can. But the cork and rubber ball—about the size of a snooker ball, though only slightly harder than a squash ball—loses speed with every rebound or bounce. Henry and she are able to return most of the shots and soon their larger opponents' grunts of effort become oaths of frustration. The winning shot is the first to land in the dead man's hole; in a desperate attempt to reach the ball Sebastian dives towards it but only succeeds in tripping over the step.

Sebastian glares at her as another pair enters the court. Clearly he is considering some kind of retaliation that will take place outside the game, though he is not the kind of person to wait for revenge to be served cold.

Sure enough, it is after showering that she hears Sebastian calling out to her from the boys' changing rooms: "Oh Arsey, oh *Arsey*! Are you looking for something?" Joan has just left the girls' lockers and her own bag has been moved. She finishes buttoning her blouse and walks straight into the boys', where Sebastian is standing next to a toilet. The toilet seat is up and a small group of boys have gathered around to watch. She hears Joan sidle in behind her.

"Hello, Arsey," Sebastian smirks. "I have a dilemma for you. In my left hand I hold your wallet, which I'm guessing has a very small amount of money and your precious library card. In my right hand, I hold Henry's school diary. Below them is a recently used toilet, which—" he sniffs "—has not yet been flushed."

She rebukes herself for not predicting this course of events. Of course Sebastian and Joan would go straight for the most obvious target: theft and damage to property. The notes in the wallet are paper but can be cleaned; the various cards are plastic. The wallet itself has some modest sentimental value as a gift from Mother, but it could also be salvaged. The diary, if dropped, will be ruined. She moves to stand next to the toilet, opposite Sebastian, sizing him up. She is faster than the overweight boy, but snatching either item back will still be difficult. Probably one, perhaps both, would fall into the toilet. Unfortunate.

"Here's the dilemma," Sebastian is giggling. "If you do nothing, Henry's diary is on a track going straight into the toilet. But if you say a word, any word, then you'll save Henry's diary—though it will then be your wallet that goes in the loo. So what's it going to be? I'll count down from five, and if you say nothing then I know you want the diary to go in the loo. Ready? Five."

How quick are his reactions? Misdirection could work—suggesting that Sebastian's trousers are not properly done up, for example. Or reference to the pornography that he keeps in his locker. But he may drop the wallet before registering the meaning.

"Four."

The other boys are getting excited. There is no time to call for help. Henry is now standing next to her. There are no cameras in the bathrooms.

"Three."

Is Sebastian bluffing? Probably not. The grin on his face shows his enjoyment of the situation and he will not let the audience go without some kind of denouement.

"Two."

Action required then. There is sufficient space, but she must be quick or both items will be dropped.

"On—" The syllable is only being formed when her fist connects with the larger boy's face. Sebastian staggers back, diary and wallet still in his hands—but as a precaution she has already kicked the lid of the toilet down. The room falls silent, uncertain as to Sebastian's reaction. His eyes are watering and blood begins to drip from his nose, which she has hit hard enough to bloody but not to break.

Taking the advantage of a few seconds of shock, she takes the wallet and returns the diary to Henry, who accepts it without a word. Sebastian's hands go to his nose, staunching the bleeding and feeling to check that it is still in the centre of his face.

Shock is followed by pain; pain by anger. She has walked past Joan to the door of the change rooms but hears the roar behind her as Sebastian recovers. She turns to face the larger boy as he runs, blood now streaming down his face, towards her. What skill he lacks in Fives he makes up for in the brawn he brings to rugby. She braces herself for the coming tackle, but at the last moment he pulls up short, stopping less than three feet away.

"Go to Headmaster, Arcadia," Mr. Ormiston is standing behind her and has seen enough. "Now."

5
DETAINED

"Come in, Miss Greentree."

She has not been back in this office in more than three years. As on the previous occasion, Headmaster does not look up from the file he is reading but gestures vaguely towards the single chair opposite his desk.

"Why are you here?"

The oak desk is unchanged, though no colourful boxes are on the agenda for this morning. The bookshelves lining the left side of the room have a few new volumes and the carpet at the base of one end is scuffed. Otherwise the room looks the same as it did during her unusual interview. Headmaster himself is ageless: having embraced white hair some years ago, it masks the toll that time now takes. The slight mussing of the hair over his right ear indicates a recent conversation on the telephone.

"As Mr. Ormiston has just told you on the telephone,

I struck Sebastian Harker. Would you care to know the context?"

"Not particularly. I'm sure he deserved it."

Unexpected. The school's approach to discipline is typically limited either to deterrence through fear of punishment or rehabilitation through moral suasion. Mr. Pratt tends towards the former, Mr. Ormiston towards the latter. But this is something new.

"Miss Greentree, let me rephrase the question. Why are you at school?" He continues to pretend to be absorbed in the papers before him, but a slight inclination of the head shows that his attention is on her. Another test?

The law requires her to be in full-time education until the age of eighteen, although home education is an option. A boring answer. To learn? Boring as well as incorrect: her accumulation of knowledge would be far greater if she were simply given the run of a decent library, a laboratory, and high-speed Internet access. A curriculum designed to shepherd a group of boys and girls whose natural abilities varies so greatly is an inefficient way of learning. Is Headmaster fishing for something else? A candle. A spark.

"Because you saw potential in me?"

A stiffening of Headmaster's shoulders shows that this is not what he wanted to hear. He takes the golden letter opener on his desk and slices open an envelope with a practised sweep, delicately removing the letter inside. "You are pandering to me, Miss Greentree. I would appreciate it if we could be honest with one another in our discussions."

Interesting. As before, he does not condescend when speaking to her. So, honesty then.

"Socialisation."

The stiffening of his shoulders relaxes. "Go on."

"School offers, of course, an education in the narrow sense of the word. But most of the curriculum could be completed by a motivated student with basic resources." The books on the shelf range from works of fiction to educational theory; the more recent additions include works on evolutionary psychology and genetic engineering. "Ideally, school develops the capacity to learn independently also—but once a baseline ability with language and certain technical skills have been achieved then most of human knowledge is attainable. I suppose one could more pretentiously say that the aim is to inculcate a lifelong love of learning, though for some of my peers that looks to be an uphill battle. In my own case, the curriculum is of course occasionally of interest and access to the laboratory and other facilities is superior to what I would have at home. But none of these really seem to apply." She returns her attention to Headmaster. "So I fall back on the idea that a primary purpose of my being here is not so much to learn how to think as how to live in a society of diverse people with diverse abilities and interests."

He still has not looked up at her. The scuffing of the carpet near the bookshelf marks out an arc from a circle.

"And how do you think you have been doing in this area?"

Socratic reasoning? Headmaster is planning to lead her through a series of questions whereby she will teach herself the moral lesson for the morning, it seems. So, moral suasion after all.

"Well the environment here is somewhat artificial, of course. Predominantly male, white, upper-middle to upper class. The Priory School socialises one for a particular stratum of society. It is possible to supplement this through getting to know the cleaning and kitchen staff—many of whom are quite knowledgeable about the realities of life. But most students barely see them, let alone talk to them."

Another signature on another file. "I asked how *you* were doing in this area."

The curve on the carpet suggests a hinge. But there would also have to be a locking mechanism, or some kind of latch.

"I confess that the emotional responses of some of my peers—and some of your teachers—can be difficult to predict. I know that I am not the most likeable person, but I get along tolerably with many of them. I understand what is expected of me in polite society. And yes, I know that physical violence is frowned upon."

He at last looks up at her, with eyes that betray a surprising weariness. "Do you ever wonder why I do not teach, Arcadia?"

Of course she has. The Priory School is not large, but Headmaster remains a distant figure. He clearly cultivates

this image much as he cultivates his hair. Such distance creates more of an impact in rare intimate moments like this. But there is more than that.

"Yes," she answers. "You used to teach science at Radley, even when you were Sub-Warden. Why did you stop?"

"Why do you think?"

"It is not a lack of ability—you appear to be in reasonable physical and mental health, and the curriculum would hardly stretch either of those. Time could be a factor; your role as Headmaster must take up a significant amount of the day. But that would explain a reduced load, not failing to teach at all. I presume it isn't that you dislike being in a school environment, or else you would consider leaving. So there is some positive reason why you choose not to teach, some benefit to maintaining this distant relationship with your students. Beyond the modest impact on discipline for them it is hard to see how this benefits them. So it must be a benefit to you, somehow."

"Close." He moves another file into his drawer, leaving only a manila folder on his desk.

A benefit to himself. There is no question of his commitment to the school and his work ethic. But what benefit comes from having so little to do with his charges? Distance reduces the opportunities to engage with students directly and understand them as individuals. But in place of that subjective relationship, maintaining distance allows a certain—

"Objectivity."

Headmaster's lip twitches upwards for the first time in this meeting. "Precisely. To be objective requires a certain detachment. In this way, I manage the school and offer an environment in which all our boys — and girls — can develop to their fullest potential. That detachment does not mean that we do not follow our students' progress closely. On the contrary. But unlike the blunt instrument of standardised testing that now obsesses much of the educational establishment, we use more sophisticated techniques."

Objectivity, but for what purpose? Did Henry have a similar conversation with Headmaster on Friday? If the bookshelf swings open, the opening mechanism is probably concealed on the shelf itself. A concealed latch, perhaps.

"In your case, for example," he continues, "you progress well in all the academic disciplines. Mr. Ormiston can be a bit melodramatic in his assessment, as you know. But outside of books you need to learn self-control. The Priory School is a safe environment, but after you complete sixth form you will be going out into a wider world and will need to harness your intellect as well as your passions."

"I did not lose my temper today."

"That is not what I said. You are an unusual young woman, Arcadia. You have certain gifts. It would be preferable to control them effectively, lest they come to control you. Do you understand?"

"Yes, sir."

"Very well. I think you do. Now, as it happens I have

one other item I would like to discuss with you. I gather from Mr. Ormiston that you still enjoy puzzles. As it happens, I have come across something that might pique your interest as well as being of service to the school."

He pats the manila folder on his desk. "We will come to this momentarily. But it is a long time since we chatted and you had such a novel approach to the three box problem. I hope you will indulge me if I offer you two, shall we say, 'warm-up questions'?"

It is a very curious disciplinary meeting, but she is not really in a position to decline. She nods her assent.

"Good," he says. "So the first question is from a grand tradition in lateral thinking: the matchstick puzzle. Sometimes they are geometrical, with one or more shapes to be manipulated by moving matchsticks. For myself, I tend to enjoy the mathematical variety and the one I have for you is in that vein."

Like an excited schoolboy himself, Headmaster reaches into a drawer and takes out a handful of matches. Using them, he lays them on the desk before her in the following arrangement:

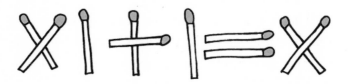

"You are familiar, of course, with Roman numerals," Headmaster says. "So this equation XI + I = X would read 'eleven plus one equals ten'. Eleven plus one obviously does *not* equal ten, so it is incorrect. Your task is to make a valid equation with the minimum movement of matchsticks. For example, one could add two more matchsticks to the 'X' on the right hand side and it would read 'eleven plus one equals twelve'. But perhaps you can find a more elegant solution?"

Deceptively simple. Moving the first vertical match — the "I" from "XI" — onto the other side would make X + I = XI. Slightly less movement would be simply to remove the vertical match from the plus sign, making XI – I = X. But that is hardly "elegant". Unless…

"Done." She announces.

Headmaster raises an eyebrow.

She smiles. "A nice puzzle, which can be completed without touching a single matchstick. One merely needs to turn the equation upside down — or switch to your side of the desk — and it reads: 'X = I + IX', or 'ten equals one plus nine'."

"Very good," he says, "but a comparatively simple puzzle. Here is a more complex one. I will write down a series of numbers. Your task is to identify the next number in the sequence." He takes a sheet of paper from the drawer of his desk and proceeds to write the following sequence of numbers, passing it to her:

2, 4, 6, 30, 32, 34, 36, 40, 42, 44, 46, 50, 52, 54, 56, 60, 62, 64, 66, ___

Interesting. An ascending sequence, but not linear. Not geometric either, as the intervals rise and fall. A pattern nonetheless, certain numbers ending in two, four, six, and zero. Though of course zero itself is not included. And at thirty, forty, fifty, and sixty the zero is not articulated...

"Two thousand."

Now both eyebrows go up. "You are sure?"

"Yes, sir. These are all numbers without the letter 'e' in them. After sixty-six, the next such number is two thousand."

"Excellent," Headmaster smiles. "Your lateral thinking skills are progressing just as we hoped." He coughs and picks up the manila folder on the desk before him. "And now perhaps we may turn to the matter of which I spoke?"

Again, she nods and Headmaster continues. "As you know, the storied history of this school includes many noteworthy alumni. I shall need to be discreet, but among these are two of the heirs to King Edward's Chair."

"The Throne of England," she murmurs. It is common knowledge that the sons of Prince Charles and Lady Diana—second and fifth in line to succeed Queen Elizabeth II—both went to the Priory School.

"Indeed. The two in question have long since graduated and their achievements are testimony, I like to think, to the upbringing of which our school played a small part. This is a source of enormous pride for all of us here. Recently, however, I chanced upon a document that has caused me some concern."

It is odd for Headmaster to confide in her in this way—unless the information could become public soon. Something sufficiently newsworthy and linked to the House of Windsor. Something that would bring the Priory School into disrepute. Given the subsequent behaviour of at least one of the heirs, it is not likely that a youthful indiscretion at school would rise to this level. It had to be something far graver.

"You think that it might somehow cast doubt upon the parentage of an heir to the throne?"

A slight widening of the eyes shows her that she is correct, but it is the only outward sign. Headmaster quickly composes himself. "I think nothing. But as you know it is customary for our students to send and receive letters once a week. In the case of one of our distinguished alumni, several of those letters from—shall we say, a non-family member—went missing."

One document found, several letters missing. "And you think this document might somehow lead you to the missing letters? To be honest, Headmaster, it sounds like a bit of a wild goose chase. The rumours about the father of the fifth in line to the throne are well-known and well-debunked. Even if there is a stash of letters from a certain captain in the army, do you not think that you might be overreacting?"

"Perhaps. But humour me and have a look at this." Headmaster slides the manila folder over towards her.

Inside are two plastic document sleeves. The first holds

a brown envelope, a generic piece of stationery available from the school's bookstore, now discoloured by dust and mildew, on which a short phrase has been printed: "The Heir Apparent's Ritual." Inside the second sleeve is a sheet of A4 paper—again, generic printer paper available at school—on which twelve lines have been printed using a laser printer and a standard font. The sheet of paper has been folded, presumably to be put into the envelope. But from the creases on the paper it has been folded first in half and then the two ends have been folded back out towards the central crease. The effect would have been that upon opening the envelope the paper would have resembled a zig-zag, or a W. Or an M.

"Where was this found?" she asks.

"In the ventilation duct of a bedroom on the third floor of the dormitory building. I think you know which room."

Yes, the one nearest the fire escape, in which the outlines of a door to an adjoining smaller bedroom for a bodyguard were still visible. "When?"

"Two weeks ago. There had been a leak in the roof and the ventilation duct was being inspected for water damage. The workers found this and it was brought to me."

"The envelope is of a kind that has been on sale at the school bookstore for as long as I have been at the Priory School. Have you tried to date it?"

"That would be difficult without the proper equipment. The style of envelope has been in use for decades."

She looks at the text on the paper inside. A curious passage that is half poem, half treasure map:

The Heir Apparent's Ritual
"Whose was it?"
"His who is gone."
"Who shall have it?"
"He who will come."
"Where was the sun?"
"At the end of the isle."
"On whom did he gaze?"
"He gazed on the knave."
"How was it stepped?"
"North by ten and by ten, east by five and by five, south by two and by two, west by one and by one, and so under."

Clearly something is hidden in this odd piece of dialogue, but what and where? The steps are fairly obvious — though a little overcomplicated since north and south, as well as east and west would cancel each other out to leave sixteen steps north and eight steps east. But starting from where? And why was the sun personified as a he? In Greek and Roman mythology, the sun god is male — Helios and Sol Invictus. But in Norse and Germanic myths the sun is a goddess. Here did it mean the literal sun, shining on the end of the island of Britain? Or onto a knave, perhaps some kind of statue of a fool, or

was it a reference to a playing card? Where could one find the sun at the end of an isle?

And hidden by whom, for whom? The "Heir Apparent"—a term referring to the *next* in line for the throne, not the second or the fifth in succession. Surely Headmaster must understand this. Unless he does. Of course he does. But the folded paper resembles an M. That speaks volumes. Of course it speaks.

She scratches her head. "I'm sorry, sir. Clearly it is a set of instructions to find something that belonged to someone who was here, but I don't see from where you would start. Did the school ever have a sundial?"

Headmaster's eyes narrow slightly; he suspects something but is not sure. "Not to my knowledge," he says after a pause.

"Or might it mean a flagpole? It is a stretch, but the 'knave' could be the jack in the Union Jack. Perhaps it is a reference to the shadow cast by the school flagpole?" The pole rises from a concrete base next to the entrance to the sports field.

"Perhaps." Headmaster seems to accept this theory. "Though we have little information about when the shadow is being cast. The sun at the end of the isle could mean the start or the end of the day, but in the course of a year the shadow would move by several yards."

"There was nothing else in the envelope?"

"Nothing."

Again she scratches her head, hoping that the gesture

does not appear too contrived. "I suppose you could start looking around the flagpole for a suitable location, though that could mean digging up much of the oval. I'm sorry that I can't be more help."

"So am I, Miss Greentree. So am I."

There is a knock on the door and Headmaster's secretary opens it. He scowls. "I said I did not want to be interrupted, Miss Bennett."

"Yes, Mr. Milton. I do apologise but we received a call from the police and I thought you might want to speak with them. Should I transfer it?"

Headmaster stands up. "No, you'll just as likely lose the call as you did last time. I'll come out." He turns to her. "We are not quite finished, Miss Greentree. Please wait there."

The door is left ajar, but once he is out of sight she stands and examines the bookshelf more closely. Henry's conversation with Headmaster on Friday that led him to run away and now this artifice about a letter that cannot possibly be about an heir to the throne — though she has a working hypothesis as to whom it does come from. And in the meantime there is the bookshelf. From the scuff marks it is the last section that must be designed to swing out. There is no sign of a latch underneath any of the shelves so she looks carefully at the books until she finds one with a dark patch of residue on its top edge from being pulled back by an index finger. As she reaches up to repeat the action, she examines the spine: a hardback edition of George Orwell's dystopian novel *Nineteen Eighty-Four*.

She gently draws the book away from the shelf and a cable releases the latch, allowing the leftmost unit of the bookshelf to swing open on well-oiled hinges.

The slight scuffing of the carpet is the only sound as she peers into the darkened space beyond. This is soon replaced by the soft hum of computers and monitors. The room is almost as big as the office it adjoins, but it is windowless and appears to have no other exit. A ventilation fan recycles the air, though without fully removing the heavy odour of electricity and heated plastic. To the left is a bank of filing cabinets. To the right is a wall of flat-screen monitors, covering a space twelve feet across from floor to ceiling. Each screen is divided into squares that show a different part of the school, making up a ten-by-ten grid of a hundred cameras feeding—live, evidently—directly into this room. A series of computer servers stands next to the screens, suggesting that recordings are being stored. In the centre of the room is a chair and table with a laptop computer and a printer.

The cameras around the school, secreted in their dark hemispheres, are not exactly hidden. But the feed would normally be expected to go to a security desk rather than to Headmaster himself. She is about to look more closely at the chair when she observes that the top-left image shows the secretary's desk outside. Headmaster is putting down the handset of the telephone and so she quickly steps back into the office proper, quietly sliding the bookshelf back into place, restoring *Nineteen Eighty-Four* to its proper angle, and returning to her chair just as the door to the office swings open.

Headmaster pauses only for a second as he enters, glancing at the bookshelf before returning his attention to her. "That was the police. It appears that there has been a break-in at your home. They had been unable to contact your parents, but we have now done so. Your mother and father are coming to collect you. I'm not sure that is necessary, but in any event they will be here in twenty minutes."

He pauses and a hand straightens the white hair behind his ear, moved out of place once more by the telephone. Another glance at the bookshelf. Does he smell the heated plastic from within his secret office? "Perhaps when you go home you might find that someone has intruded where they should not have," he says slowly. "Opening doors that had best remain closed. I do hope that you don't find this too distressing."

"Yes, sir."

"You may leave now. Oh, and on the first matter we discussed: for form's sake I would appreciate it if you could find it within yourself to apologise to Master Harker — and to inform him that you were suitably disciplined?"

"I will, sir."

"Very well." A final glance at the bookshelf then back at her. "That is all."

From Headmaster's office, she walks back towards Hall and into Chapel. The school chaplain is preparing for a service later in the day. He notices her and walks across to offer a greeting.

"Welcome, Arcadia," he smiles. "It isn't often that we see you here outside of Friday morning prayers. Is everything all right?"

"Actually, Mr. Roundhay, I've had some rather bad news. Someone has broken into our home. My parents are on the way to collect me now." Her face assumes an expression of anxiety and concern.

"My dear girl, that's terrible. But no one was injured?"

"I don't think anyone was home. But it is very upsetting."

"I can only imagine. Well as Proverbs tells us: 'Trust in the Lord with all thine heart.' At moments like these, prayer can be a great comfort. Would you like me to pray with you?"

"That's very kind of you, Father, but I wondered if I might have a moment alone with the Lord?"

"Of course, my child. I need to collect some candles from the storeroom anyway. God be with you."

She kneels at a pew in the empty Chapel until the chaplain's footsteps have faded. Then looks up at the crucifix on the wall above the altar at the end of the aisle, from which Christ the son looks down upon the nave. Proverbs is an apposite scriptural reference, as it continues: "lean not unto thine own understanding. In all thy ways acknowledge him, and he shall direct thy paths."

The quotation marks in Headmaster's riddle bothered her at first, until she realised that they indicated the words were to be said aloud. Add the fact that the letter was folded into an "M" and the puns were fairly clear: sun-son, isle-aisle, knave-nave. Now it is simply a matter of counting out the steps.

The crucifix is on the eastern wall of Chapel. But how long were the steps to be? Square paving stones on the ground offer the most likely measure. Starting from below the crucifix, she counts out twenty to the north, bringing her to the edge of Chapel and the open door of the vestry. East by ten steps takes her into the vestry, where the chaplain, altar boys, and choristers put on their vestments for the daily school services. She has been in this room only once on a tour of the school, but knows of other students who make it a significant part of their lives. South by four more paving stones brings her to the wall of the vestry and back west by two steps finds her in a corner of the room behind the east wall of Chapel.

"And so under," she whispers to herself. The paving stone on which she finds herself would be impossible for her to lift without tools, but crouching down on the ground she begins to examine the bricks in the adjacent wall. Tapping each one, she soon locates a half-brick that is loose enough to ease out of the wall. It reveals a cavity, large enough for her to reach into. Inside she finds not a bundle of letters but a small object wrapped in a dusty piece of cloth. She unwraps it to reveal a piece of carved

metal, the bow at one end reminiscent of a *fleur-de-lis* connected to a toothed blade: a key.

She quickly pockets the key, replaces the brick, and returns to the pew. Only when she hears the chaplain returning with his candles does she rise. Crossing herself for good form.

"Did you find what you were looking for?" the chaplain asks her kindly.

"I'm not sure," she replies. "But I'll keep looking."

6
BREAK-IN

She turns the key over in her pocket as she stands at the school gate, waiting for her parents. The key itself is unremarkable, designed for a pin tumbler lock with grooves down the side and a row of uneven teeth. From a quick inspection it is the same brand as the locks used at school, though she has not yet had a chance to try it on any doors. Engraving on the bow sometimes offers an indication of the use of such a key, but in this case it simply has one letter carved into the metal: an "M". Coincidence? Probably.

She waves to Father as their car turns into the school grounds. Mother climbs out to give her a hug; she is clearly distressed but trying to put on a brave face.

"It's such an awful business," Mother says to fill the silence.

As they begin the drive home, she quickly establishes that little is known. Mother had been out shopping, Father

at his clinic but busy with a patient. Some enterprising police officer thought to contact the school to reach their daughter.

"You haven't been home yet?"

"No, Arky," Mother replies. "Your father wanted to stay together. We thought you had best come with us rather than take a taxi."

"Have the police told you anything more?"

"It was chance that anyone saw the break-in at all. Mrs. Pike happened to be walking her dog and saw a teenager near the house," Father says, eyes still on the road. "She thought it might have been you until he hopped over the gate. Mrs. Pike has always been a bit nosey, and when she peeked in the window she saw him sneaking about inside. That's when she called the police. Thank goodness for the old busy-body!"

"Now Ignatius, we should be grateful to Mrs. Pike," Mother scolds him gently. "But for her the thief might have taken far more."

"Do we know what was taken?" Arcadia asks.

"The police said the telly was gone, but apart from that they aren't sure. That's why they want us to take a look around."

"Here we are," says Father, pulling into their driveway.

A police van is parked by the side of the road, but the house is quiet. They enter through the front door and much of their home seems untouched. The carpet suggests recent traffic moving across it, but a police officer's shoes have trampled over what might have been the intruder's footprints.

It is only the living room that has obviously been disturbed. In addition to taking the television, the drawer from the desk by the telephone has been emptied onto the floor and various items on the mantelpiece have been knocked down—broken glass from a vase is scattered across the floor. But it looks more like someone making a mess than searching for valuables. The back door is intact and locked once more. She examines it from the outside. Not even a scratch.

Mother is fiddling with her mobile phone and Father is surveying the damage. She moves upstairs to her own room. Though unlikely to be regarded by anyone as tidy, it is orderly with its piles of papers and half-completed experiments. The police do not appear to have been inside, but someone else has. It takes her a few minutes to identify the signs, as the intruder was very careful. No obvious disturbance of the carpet or the items in the room, but there is something.

Or rather there is nothing. No dust. She looks across the tops of the magazines and specimen jars and sees that the dust that had been accumulating for some weeks is now gone. Mother occasionally asks her to clean her room, but she would not go in without asking her. For an intruder, dust is almost impossible to replace—once disturbed, it was simpler to clean the room rather than try to restore it. Someone has carefully gone through her

room, putting everything in its proper location except the dust that once covered it. Curious.

She sits down on her bed. Downstairs, the doorbell rings and she hears her parents invite a police officer inside. Three pairs of footsteps ascend the stairs. Her back is to the open door of her room but a faint smell of coconut oil precedes the policeman.

"Constable Lestrange," she says before turning around. "I wasn't expecting to see you quite so soon."

"You two know each other?" Father asks.

"Indeed," she replies, standing up. "Don't you recall that he was the officer at the school gate when you dropped me off yesterday?"

"Of course he was. Sorry, Constable, it's been a bit of a stressful day."

"Not at all," says the officer. "Now, have you established what is missing?"

"So far just the television." Father leads them back downstairs. "My wife and I have a safe in the bedroom, but it hasn't been touched. There were some coins on the dressing table — they're still there. We'll need a little while to see if anything else has been taken, but there isn't actually that much of value."

"Have you noticed anything missing, Arky?" Mother asks, still frowning at her phone. "You have good eyes for that sort of thing."

"Missing? No. Though it would be worth looking around nearby rubbish bins to see if the television turns up." She pauses. "The thief might have had a change of heart."

"Oh, this blasted thing!" Mother mutters, putting her phone on the table.

"What's wrong?"

"I'm trying to get hold of Magnus and the phone isn't working."

"There's been some kind of interference recently," Constable Lestrange says. "The police radio has been acting up also."

"Let me call him on the landline for you." She dials Magnus's mobile number and waits until her brother finally picks up the phone after the sixth ring.

"Yes?"

"Hello, brother dear."

"Why, Arcadia, what an unexpected pleasure," Magnus's languid voice intones. "Are the police still there?"

"Yes."

"Aren't you going to ask how I knew the police were there?"

"It's one officer, and no I wasn't planning to ask."

"Simple deduction: my caller ID shows that it is a phone call from our home and yet it is my sister calling me on a school day. Trouble, clearly, but not of the kind that takes you to a hospital. Ergo an incident at the house, I'm guessing theft and/or property damage. Correct?"

"Remind me, Magnus, this graduate degree you are now pursuing at Cambridge: is it a doctorate in stating the obvious?"

"Oh very droll, Arcadia. I suppose Mother wants to speak with me?"

"Yes, but first I wanted to thank you."

"Oh?"

"For the key."

"Ah." There is a slight squeak of leather on the other end of the line as her brother shifts his prodigious weight, probably in an overstuffed chair in his college's common room. "Not bad, Arcadia. It only took you three years."

She knows better than to ask what the key opens.

"Don't tell me you are going to ask what the key unlocks," Magnus purrs down the line.

"Of course not. But I was curious if there were in fact any missing letters — or was that merely a rumour that you had started yourself?"

"Come, come, sister dear. You know what a staunch monarchist I am. I would never stoop to dishonourable rumour-mongering."

"So there *were* letters. But you would only plant your own message and the key if you knew that the letters were safe, or destroyed. When did you find the original letters?"

"When I was in remove in second year. I was visiting in the room formerly occupied by our distinguished alumnus and observed that the air coming through the ventilation duct was flowing inconsistently. At an opportune time I opened the duct and found a stack of letters to the former student. They were all addressed with the same male hand, postmarked from London. The fact that they lacked a return address but had been carefully kept indicated a close but secret personal relationship.

"I discreetly reached out to the, er, family—not a simple thing at the age of fourteen—and offered to return the letters or burn them. A car was ultimately sent with a man who collected them. They asked if I would care for a reward but I declined. It was my patriotic duty, I said."

"And you didn't read the letters."

"Perish the thought, Arcadia. These were private. And, more importantly, they were Royal."

"So the little puzzle you left for me—I am, presumably, the heir apparent?"

"Naturally: 'He who will come.' It would have been a little too obvious to say '*She* who will come.' In any case, as you know, the Queen is occasionally made an honorary man in order to enter certain of London's more traditional clubs." He paused. "Though I suppose if someone else had found the message and the key then *he* would have been my true heir. Yet I always had high hopes that it would be you, Arcadia."

"How very fraternal of you."

"Well, Mother does always tell me to look after you."

"Speaking of Mother, she does want a word with you. But there is one last thing I wanted to ask."

"Hmm?"

"On the placement of the key itself, I hadn't realised that you had such an interest in Chapel. Is there something I don't know about you?"

"Why Arcadia, what you don't know about me could fill volumes."

Mother insists that she have lunch with them before returning to school. She prepares some sandwiches while her daughter lays the table. The doorbell rings and she opens it for Constable Lestrange, who has returned from some further investigation.

"Would you care for a sandwich, Constable?" Mother asks, ever hospitable.

"No thanks, Ma'am. I have good news and bad news for you on the television."

If the bad news is that it's broken then finding it hardly constitutes good news, but she holds her tongue.

"The good news is that we found your television. It was in a skip on a building site two streets down. The bad news is that it is most likely damaged beyond repair. It seems the thief got tired of carrying it or was worried about being caught and threw it in the skip. The screen is cracked and some parts have fallen out. I am sorry about that."

"Well, thank you for letting us know," Mother says. "Can I at least get you a cup of tea?"

"That would be grand. White and one sugar, please."

"Do you think it's odd?" Arcadia asks.

"What, lass?"

"Someone breaks in here without leaving a mark on the door. He walks around much of the house. Messes up one room, takes one thing, and then abandons it two streets away. This is a decidedly atypical burglar, highly skilled, but with no obvious motive."

"Well I'm getting bars put on the windows this weekend," Mother announces, giving Constable Lestrange his cup of tea.

The officer takes a sip. "Often you can't tell with teenagers. They don't always act rationally." He glances at Arcadia and clears his throat. "Well, *most* of them don't act rationally. Maybe this kid was looking for money or drugs and then got spooked. He grabbed the most expensive thing to hand and legged it. A teenager walking around carrying a TV is going to stand out, though, so he decided to dump it and call it a day."

"Possibly." But she is unconvinced. The mess in the living room is too contained. It is also the room through which the intruder entered and left the house. He would not have wanted to make so much noise at the beginning, so it must have been at the end. Someone carefully went through the house, but then at the last moment attempted to make it look like a burglary. Why?

Constable Lestrange soon finishes his tea and stands up. "Thank you for the tea, Ma'am, but I'd best get back to the station. We've got you and your husband's statements, but if you have any questions please don't hesitate to contact us. Oh, and we did dust for fingerprints around the door, but our intruder appears to have worn gloves. I'm sorry I can't be more help."

Arcadia walks him to the front door. "Thank you, Constable Lestrange."

"Only doing my job, lass." He hesitates, then takes a card from his pocket and writes a number on the back. "This is my mobile number in case you think of anything that might help."

She pockets the card and closes the door.

A thief who breaks in, moves carefully around the house, and then — is interrupted? He did not expect to be seen and then quickly had to create an explanation for the break-in, making it look like a burglary. But what was the original intent? Not to take a television, surely.

Looking for something else? Nothing appeared to be missing.

Or leaving something behind?

She returns to the foyer and looks more carefully at the marks on the carpet. In addition to a jumble of footprints, four small squares are identifiable on the carpet adjacent to the hat stand, forming the corners of a larger square about a foot wide. A chair? From the dining table she carries a chair back to the foyer. The four legs fit precisely into the imprints.

An intruder would not position a chair in a hallway in order to sit. She stands on top of the chair, head now above the hat stand by the door and almost touching the metal light fitting that hangs from the ceiling. She turns around, trying to imagine what interest the intruder could have had in the ceiling.

It is so small that she almost misses it, a piece of black plastic only slightly larger than a matchstick attached with invisible tape to one of the bars of the light fitting. A slim cord runs up the bar and behind the lightshade where it plugs into a black cube two inches square and an inch deep. A power source and transmitter for the tiny camera that now peers out on the entrance to their home.

She is looking at the camera from the side, meaning that she has probably not come into its field of vision. She climbs back down and takes the chair in the direction of the dining table, scanning the carpet as she walks, but without moving her head. Two more sets of indentations help her locate cameras that have been placed on top of the bookshelf facing the living room and in another light fitting in the dining room itself. Upstairs, in her own room, it takes a little longer as she must pretend to be looking for something else, but she soon finds a camera concealed on top of her wardrobe. There are probably more.

The cameras are sophisticated. What would a teenager be doing planting them in her parents' home? She contemplates telling Mother and Father immediately, but knows that their reaction would be to leave the house at once or start tearing down the cameras.

Could there be some connection to the elaborate surveillance network at the Priory School? This seems

implausible. But who would bother to go to such lengths to spy on a family like hers?

She needs more information and at present the best way to gather it is to leave the cameras in place. For the moment, then, she will say nothing—at least until she is able to confer with Magnus. That will have to wait until she is back at school, however, as she must now assume that the house telephone is bugged also. Before then, she will do a little more investigating of her own.

"Good afternoon, Mrs. Pike. How are you today?" She offers her most winning smile when their elderly neighbour answers her knock.

"Oh, can't complain, young Arcadia," Mrs. Pike replies, opening the door for her. "Would you like to come in?" An asthmatic bulldog bounds towards the door from the hallway inside, but she blocks its path with her foot. It breathes heavily, tongue dangling from one side of its mouth.

"That's very kind of you, but I've got to get back to school. The police told us what a courageous thing you did. I just wanted to say thank you."

Through the layers of makeup she cannot be sure, but the older woman appears to blush. "No bother, no bother. Have they caught the rapscallion?"

"Alas no," she sighs. "Your description was very

helpful, however. They said it had given them a good shot at catching the, uh, rapscallion."

"Good, good," she nods.

"If you aren't too exhausted by the episode, would you be able to tell me what happened? It's ever so exciting." She blinks her eyes enthusiastically, trying not to overdo it.

It has the desired effect. "To be honest," Mrs. Pike begins, "I didn't get much of a look at him when he was loitering around your front door. Then he went and climbed over your gate. At first I thought he was you! Forgive me dear — you can't tell boys from girls with these baggy clothes that children wear these days. Winston and I were on our walk to the park — you know my Winston" she scratches behind the ear of the bulldog wheezing at her feet — "he loves his walks does Winston. But then I said to Winston, 'Young Arcadia is at school!' I said. 'And why would she be hanging about outside her own front door and jumping over fences?' So, on our way back I popped over for a closer look. The lights were out and he was skulking about inside. This was passing strange, so Winston and I crept over to see what kind of funny business he was up to. My guess is that he knew your pa was a doctor and he was after some of those drugs. That's what I said to the boys in blue. Anyway I couldn't see too well inside on account of the lights being off and it was a sunny day outside but it was clear he was not on the side of the angels. That's when Winston and I knew we had to call the police. Didn't we, boy?"

The bulldog's panting is taken as an affirmation. "So I took out my phone and was calling the police when I think he must have seen me. There was this terrible crash of glass and then I heard your back door open and slam. I thought he might come after us so Winston and I hurried back to our home and bolted the door. I kept an eye out on the street after that, but we saw neither hide nor hair of him. And then the police showed up — too late, as usual."

"You were very brave," Arcadia says. A pool of saliva has started to collect on the floor below Winston's chops. "Both of you."

"Oh we were just doing what any concerned citizens would do."

"Do you recall anything else about the boy? What he was wearing?"

"Like I said, I didn't really get a good look at him but he was about your height and slim like you. At first I thought he was a girl — but of course girls don't get up to this sort of mischief. What I should have done is take a photo with my phone. Oh, but every time I try to do that I end up with a picture of my finger.

"He was wearing all black: black shoes, black trousers, and one of those black sweater things with a hood over his head. Or it might have been blue. I told all this to that nice young policeman, so I do hope they catch him."

"So do I. Thank you again, Mrs. Pike."

"You're welcome dear. Give my best to your parents."

A tug on Winston's collar and the two of them disappear inside once more.

She crosses the road back to her house where her parents are preparing to drive her back to school. Mother has declared that she won't stay in the house by herself and will spend the afternoon with Father at his clinic.

"Mrs. Pike sends her best," she says as they climb into the car.

"That's sweet," says Mother. "We should drop off a cake or some flowers to thank her for sounding the alarm."

They drive in silence for a few minutes.

"I'm looking forward to your concert tomorrow night," Mother says eventually. "That should brighten up the week. And it's not like we would be home watching the telly!" She smiles to herself.

Mother abhors silence, though her daughter has always been comfortable in it. To be alone with one's thoughts can be a frightening or a liberating thing. Liberating if it opens up vistas of knowledge and the potential for understanding. Frightening if it underscores the reality that we are each ultimately and irrevocably alone.

Mother's finger is poised over the radio but she decides against turning it on. "Arky," she continues, "you're growing up so fast now. I mean, you were always very mature for your age, but now you're becoming a woman."

Where is this going—not sex education in the car, surely? Yet her tone is different. Mother has something more serious on her mind.

"As you get older, you get more responsibilities—you know that. But you also find out more about the world, about your place in it. And you have to work out where you stand. Sometimes this can be difficult. That's true for children but it's also true for parents."

She is struggling for the right words. "You know your father and I love you very much."

"Of course."

"And we would never do anything to put you in danger. But we won't always be able to protect you. I'm not sure we protect you that much now. Because sometimes parents can't control everything that affect their children. That's when, as a parent, you have to hope that you've done enough that your kids can protect themselves."

She is telling the truth but being evasive. What is she worried about? Something more than the break-in.

The silence resumes until this time it is Father who interrupts it. "What Louisa is trying to say is that if anything ever happens to us, you and Magnus will need to look after each other. I know you two don't always get on, but you're family and sometimes that's all you can hang onto."

"I understand," she says.

But she does not.

"My dear sister, two calls in a day. Are you suddenly becoming sentimental?"

"No more than you, Magnus. But I thought you should know a little more about today's adventure at home." She is standing at the school gate after waving off her parents. Mobile phones must be switched off on campus during school hours so she has made the call from the edge of the school grounds.

"You mean the break-in that wasn't a break-in," Magnus replies. "Have they found the television yet?"

"Yes, two streets away. I had suggested to the police that they search nearby for it."

"Oh, very well done, Arcadia. And now you're calling me to say that the real purpose wasn't actually to steal a five-year old television set but rather to...?"

"Install a surveillance system. There are at least four miniature cameras at various points in our house, from the foyer to my bedroom. Probably more."

There is silence at the other end of the phone.

"Magnus?"

"Just a minute, Arcadia. I'm afraid I didn't catch what you said as there's some interference on the phone. I should be able to fix it, but you might want to hold the phone away from your ear for a moment."

She does so just as the speaker lets out a loud burst of white noise and her phone goes dead. After a moment she sees that it has reset and is booting up once again. When it has completed the cycle she has a text message from Magnus:

> Thanks for calling Arcadia, though I must say that it was nothing new. That's all 4 the moment. 'Bye now. Magnus

"4"? Her brother really does think that she is dense. It doesn't take a Cambridge degree to work out that Magnus has included a second message within his text using every fourth word: "Arcadia, say nothing 4 (for) now."

It is unusual for her to confide in Magnus in this way, but in the area of surveillance her brother's knowledge is superior to her own. The burst of white noise was presumably some device to avoid interception, but who would be listening in on their telephone calls? Perhaps Magnus is being paranoid. Perhaps he is being prudent.

In deference to the school rule, she switches off her phone — then removes the battery and SIM card as an added precaution. She puts the disassembled device in her bag next to her Swiss Army knife and goes in search of her class, trying not to look directly at the school's security cameras as she does.

7
SUBSTITUTE

She arrives halfway through Latin. Mr. Ormiston concludes reciting the forms of the irregular verb *fio, fieri* and a nod of his head indicates that she should take her seat.

Sebastian welcomes her back with an attempt to trip her as she walks by his desk. "Why welcome back, *Arsey*," he smirks. "What did Headmaster do to you this morning? I heard that after seeing him you went straight to Chapel to pray!"

"Yes, Sebastian," she replies with mock sincerity. "I prayed to the Lord for forgiveness as I now seek it from you. I can only take comfort in the fact that my pugilism doesn't appear to have problematised your proboscis one way or the other."

As Sebastian tries to work out whether he is being insulted, Mr. Ormiston moves to stand between them. "Miss Greentree, Master Harker, I think we have had

about enough excitement from the two of you. I would appreciate it if you could resume your seats and continue your Latin without speaking. I shall be watching you both extremely closely."

"Yes, sir," the two mumble. She opens her Latin book and begins writing down the various forms of the verb "to become".

After Latin, they have a free period and Henry is heading towards the library. She catches up with him and they walk together in silence. Once inside the library, they climb the circular stairs to the second floor where the books in the high 500s of the Dewey Decimal system are located. He picks up a book about the fish of the Maldives while she chooses a monograph on the Gila monster.

Henry shifts uncomfortably when she sits down at a desk opposite him, but they read in quiet contemplation for several minutes. As fascinating as the book on the venomous American lizard is, however, she has more immediate queries to answer. She takes a blank piece of paper from her bag and writes: "Henry, I know that Headmaster is watching us and I know that he said something that upset you on Friday. What?" She passes the page to Henry, who reads it and shakes his head.

"Please," she whispers.

Henry pauses, then writes below her precise cursive

in his own hand: "He said that if I told you anything that I would be expelled. My father will kill me if that happens."

She reads this and hesitates. Henry is the closest thing she has to a friend. Though the prospects of his father actually murdering him are remote, she does not want to make the boy's life more difficult than it already is. But she needs more information to understand what is going on around her. She continues writing: "Today I found that someone has installed secret cameras in my parents' house. Do you know anything about that?"

She shows it to him; he frowns and shakes his head again. This time it is an answer to her question rather than a rejection of it. There is no reason for him to lie, so he probably has no knowledge of the cameras. But what did Headmaster say on Friday that led Henry to run away?

"Did Headmaster ask you to do something you didn't think was right?"

She holds up the page to Henry. After a quick glance around the empty second floor of the library, he nods.

"To spy on someone?" she writes.

There is a catch in his breathing. She is close.

She whispers: "On me?"

A single nod, burying his nose back in a picture of the Maldivian reefs. She folds the paper thoughtfully. "Thank you, Henry," she says softly, standing up.

After leaving the library she tears the page carefully

into small pieces, flushing portions of the shreds down two different toilets.

Returning to the dormitory building, she is about to unlock her door when she pauses, reaching into her pocket for the key that Magnus planted long ago in Chapel. Though the teeth are cut differently from her own key, she tries it in the door to her room. It fits perfectly and, though a little stiff, turns and opens the lock. She steps back into the hallway of the dormitory. Opposite her room is a storage cupboard. She tries the key there and — it opens that lock also. So "M" stands for master key.

"And thank you, Magnus," she whispers. Her situation is no clearer, but for the first time she begins to feel that she has an advantage.

The last lesson of the day is science with Mr. Pratt. She checks that the cardboard in her rear pockets is in place, just in case.

She takes her seat next to Henry. Sebastian is whispering to Joan, occasionally glancing in her direction. Some kind of tiresome plot is underway, but he will not step out of line during Mr. Pratt's lesson.

When the bell rings, however, it is their form teacher, Mr. Ormiston, who enters. Following close behind is a woman. The students stand.

The number of female staff at the Priory School can be counted on one hand. In addition to the part-time cleaners and the ladies in the canteen, there are a various female administrators such as Headmaster's secretary. Of the teaching staff, however, the women are confined to areas such as music, art, and French. The head of the art department is the only senior position held by a woman.

The disparity is usually explained as being due to tradition rather than discrimination. Nevertheless, the school's Web site lists teachers by initials and surname; men do not have a title such as "Mr." (apart from Pipe-Major Scott, the school bagpipe instructor), while women are variously identified as "Miss" and "Mrs." to indicate their gender and marital status.

The woman standing beside Mr. Ormiston is not a current member of staff. A substitute teacher for Mr. Pratt, presumably. The fact that the school has arranged a new teacher indicates that he is more than ill, but has suffered some injury that will keep him from school for at least a few weeks. What a shame. But there is something more.

"Settle down," Mr. Ormiston intones. "You may be seated. I regret to inform you that Mr. Pratt has been involved in an unfortunate motor accident. He will be fine and will be returning to school, though I am told that he is likely to remain in hospital for the next month." He pauses to clear his throat. "I can tell how concerned you all are and will be certain to pass on your best wishes for his speedy recovery.

"We are extremely fortunate, however, to have a new science teacher to fill in for Mr. Pratt while he is indisposed. This is Miss Alderman and she will be taking over your science classes for the rest of the term. I am confident that you will show her the same respect that you show to all members of our staff. Am I clear?" He looks around the room, eyes fixing on Sebastian and Arcadia in particular.

"Very well, Miss Alderman, they're all yours. You know where to find me if needed."

"Thank you, William," she smiles, touching his elbow before he departs. A little too familiar. Before going out the door, Mr. Ormiston turns back to look at her once more. Then for a second his eyes fall on Arcadia again. He hurriedly shuts the door and his footsteps disappear down the hall.

Miss Alderman turns to face them. In her mid-thirties, she is around ten years younger than Mr. Ormiston; dressed well but modestly. Her glasses and pale skin suggest bookishness, but below a knee-length dress her calves and strong shoulders indicate that she exercises regularly. Indoors, it seems. Her posture is exceptionally good—unlike Mr. Ormiston's amateur schoolboy productions, it is possible that Miss Alderman actually had some success in the theatre.

"Good morning ladies and gentlemen," she gives them a brisk smile. "I understand that you have been discussing the basics of evolution. Today we will continue with biology, but are going to discuss the genetic and environmental influences on development — what is often referred to as the relative impact of 'nature' and 'nurture'."

She turns to the board and writes: "Nature vs Nurture". "Now, who can give me an example of a characteristic or trait that is genetic or natural?"

"Being an ugly cow," Sebastian offers up, looking in Arcadia's direction and getting a snigger from some of the boys sitting near him.

She consults a list of names and photographs. "Thank you — Sebastian, is it? Yes indeed most of our physical characteristics can be attributed to our genetic heritage, from the colour of our eyes and hair to the relative length of our arms and legs." She drops her voice to a stage whisper: "Though you can't blame your appearance entirely on your parents, Sebastian. It's possible you were dropped as a baby."

Arcadia smiles to herself. She is going to like this teacher.

"What about an example of an environmental influence that could have an impact on one's development?" she continues. "Something on the 'nurture' side of the equation?"

Henry puts up his hand and she consults her sheet. "Yes, Henry?"

"Having a jerk for a father?"

"Well, I was thinking of something much more basic, like how much food we get to eat. How tall we grow depends in part on our genes, but there is great variation based on nutrition. In the course of the twentieth century, for example, the Dutch went from being Europe's shortest people to being among the tallest. This was basically due to increased wealth and better food. The average height in the Netherlands went up by around seven inches.

"Today, the United Nations uses height in order to monitor nutrition levels in developing countries. So the importance of nurture is fairly clear: if you don't eat, you don't grow.

"But yes, coming back to Henry's point, the way we are treated can have an important influence on our character. Here the mix of nature and nurture is more complicated, though. Various studies have shown that genes do have an impact on character — if you know anyone who breeds animals, you'll be aware that they routinely select for certain character traits. We generally like to think that humans are not just the sum of our DNA, however. And indeed someone who is treated badly as a child is more likely to 'inherit' those qualities as an adult.

"So we have a paradox. Agriculture and farming have depended on selective breeding for thousands of years. From our earliest forebears, farmers have chosen crops and animals with desirable qualities, tending to produce seeds and offspring that were bigger and healthier. Nature can clearly be shaped through breeding. We know also that blue-eyed parents have blue-eyed babies and so on. Yet we rarely talk about human breeding in the same way as animals. Why not?"

This is a tired debate topic that has been drilled into the class before. "The Nazis," they respond, almost in unison.

If Miss Alderman is taken aback she does her best not to show it. "Exactly. The racial policies of Nazi Germany put the whole science of eugenics — genetic improvement of the human population — into disrepute. Some eugenics policies did continue into the late twentieth century, such as the forced sterilisation of the mentally ill in Sweden and incentives for the highly-educated to have children in Singapore. But these policies were controversial and ultimately abandoned.

"Indeed, in the course of the twentieth century the idea that genes had *any* impact on human development was largely discredited. That was, of course, an overreaction.

"We are far more than our genes, to be sure. Much of the population of Australia, for example, is descended from the criminals transported there as punishment by the English — and yet today it is a reasonably law-abiding society. This would seem to argue against any strong genetic link to criminality.

"But genes clearly do play a role in many aspects of the way we grow physically — and, almost certainly, in the way we think and the way we act. But how could we test this theory? How could we measure the relative impact of nature and nurture?"

She looks around the room expectantly. "Arcadia?"

She did not consult the list to check her name. Either

she has memorised the list or she knew it already.

"Take two individuals with the same genes and raise them in different environments," Arcadia replies.

"Very good. And what do we call individuals with the same genes?"

"Clones?" Henry offers. "Like Dolly the sheep?"

"Excellent, Henry."

"Yeah," Sebastian interjects. "But I thought the Clone Wars happened a long time ago in a galaxy far, far away."

"Oh Sebastian, I can tell that you and I are going to get along famously," Miss Alderman remarks. "But you do make a good point in your accidental and indirect way: cloning humans remains controversial. So is there an easier way to test our 'nature versus nurture' theory on humans?"

"Identical twins."

"Thank you, Arcadia. Yes, identical twins share the same genes and are, essentially, clones. Now in most cases twins stay as part of a family and so nature and nurture largely influence them in similar ways. These twins will not be exactly the same, but for our purposes it would be ideal if there were identical twins who grew up in different environments.

"This is less common, but for two decades the Minnesota Study of Twins Reared Apart, or 'Mistra', scoured the globe to find such twins. From 1979 to 1999, researchers examined more than a hundred pairs of identical and non-identical twins who were separated in early childhood and raised in different households. What they found is that many characteristics thought to be entirely environmental — things like foods preferences, reading habits, even how religious someone is or their career choice — actual show strong genetic influences.

"In some cases, this produced uncanny results. Consider the case of the two Jims. Identical twins, Jim Springer and Jim Lewis, were adopted by different families at four weeks of age. They met for the first time thirty-nine years later. Yet at school, both said that mathematics had been their best subject and spelling their worst. Both smoked the same brand of cigarettes and drank the same brand of beer. In their spare time, they both did carpentry in their garage. They both drove Chevrolets and had a dog named Toy. Both had worked in law enforcement and took holidays at the same beach in Florida. They had each been married twice: first to women named Linda and then to women named Betty. Each of the Jims had a son: one was named James Allen, the other was named James Alan.

"A lot of this was coincidence. No one would seriously suggest that your genes could *make* you marry someone called Linda and then divorce her for someone called Betty. Yet it is possible that genes and our environment interact in a more complex way than we had assumed — that it is not nature *versus* nurture, but perhaps nature *via* nurture. In other words, some genes might depend on the right environment in order to be expressed. Genes are not destiny, but they may be potential."

She turns back to the board and erases the "vs" to replace it with a double-headed arrow, so that it now reads: "Nature ↔ Nurture".

"So how might we explore this more dynamic model of nature and nurture, in which variations in the environment affect the expression of our genetic potential?"

"Try out different environments?" Henry suggests.

"Indeed," Miss Alderman says. "Now, experimenting in this way on humans would be exceedingly difficult. But another group of scientists conducted experiments on rhesus monkeys in the mid-twentieth century. They were particularly interested in the relationship between mother and infant.

"At the time, many people assumed that mothers were primarily a source of nutrition and that any emotional attachment between mother and child was basically the extension of a feeding bond. So Harry Harlow and his colleagues created a test. He took the infant monkeys away from their mothers soon after birth and placed them in controlled environments. In place of their natural mothers, he offered them a," she coughs, "surrogate mother, made from wood and rubber, covered with a soft cloth and warmed with a light bulb. Despite the fact that they were not alive, the baby monkeys still learned to recognise these artificial mothers, preferring them against all others.

"In a second experiment, he offered the baby monkeys a choice of two 'mothers': one was the wood and cloth type, a second was made of wire mesh. For some of the baby monkeys, the wire model held a bottle with food. These babies stayed with the wire model only as long as it took to get the food they needed. Otherwise they would cuddle with the softer cloth model, especially when they were scared. For other baby monkeys, the cloth model had the bottle: those babies didn't pay attention to the wire model at all.

"What he was really trying to measure was love. And what he found was that love is at least as important to early primate development as food.

"These experiments were, as you might expect, controversial. More controversial still were his efforts to investigate what happened if you deprived the baby monkeys of even these surrogate mothers. For this third experiment he took infant monkeys—a few hours old—and put them in total isolation. The monkeys were fed and sheltered, but left entirely alone in a metal box for three, six, and even twelve months. Those that were isolated for three months could eventually be reintegrated into the society of other monkeys. But those isolated for longer than that were permanently damaged and never fully recovered."

"Isn't that just cruel?" Henry asks.

"Many people do think so," Miss Alderman responds. "Some even go so far as to say that his experiments started the movement to protect animals from this kind of treatment. Although his findings might seem obvious to us today, however, in the 1950s many parents were being told not to coddle their children, that too much physical contact was bad for them, and so on. Harlow's work helped show how damaging the *lack* of contact could be in monkeys—and that there was strong evidence that the same applied to humans."

Miss Alderman erases the double-headed arrow and replaces it with two question marks: "Nature ?? Nurture". "There is still a lot that we don't know," she says. "Clearly genes have a significant impact on our lives. Clearly our environment plays a role also. But human life is so varied, so unpredictable, that we will probably never be able to devise an experiment that could accurately measure all the ways in which these various factors interact to make us the complex individuals we eventually become."

Unless you could control the environment completely. And then observe everything that happens. Record it. While maintaining scientific objectivity.

At the front of the room, Miss Alderman erases the words on the board completely. "That's all for today, boys and girls. Read the rest of the chapter on evolution and I'll see you on Friday."

She is about to leave when Miss Alderman calls her over. "Arcadia, may I have a word with you?"

"Of course." She approaches the desk at the front.

"It's nice to meet you at last."

The teacher puts out her hand. An odd gesture when meeting a student, but Arcadia shakes it. Their eyes meet for a moment longer than custom would dictate. Curious.

"Mr. Ormiston mentioned that you are interested in biology," Miss Alderman says. "I studied biology at Oxford — it's a fascinating subject. The building blocks of life and so on."

Arcadia nods, buying a moment. Clears her throat. Only then raises her eyes again. "So why did you drop out?"

"Excuse me?"

"Why did you drop out of graduate study at university? You are clearly passionate about the subject and inclined to research — yet you never completed a doctorate in the subject. I'm guessing it was not a lack of ability, so you dropped out. Why?" There is surprise in the teacher's eyes. Perhaps she has touched a nerve. "I apologise if I'm intruding."

Miss Alderman laughs. "No that's all right. Mr. Ormiston warned me about this. You're perfectly entitled to ask and you are correct that I started but did not finish a doctorate. Let's say that I made a choice that wasn't compatible with doing so."

"I see," she replies. "Well I'm pleased that the time you spent acting at Oxford was more profitable."

The teacher's lips part as a frown forms on her brow. Another laugh, though a false one. "Young lady, you aren't possibly old enough to have seen any of the shows that I was in."

"Alas no," she concedes. "At least not on the stage."

Miss Alderman looks at her curiously. "All right then, off you go."

"Goodbye, Miss Alderman."
"Goodbye, Arcadia."

She leans against the wall of the classroom block, nose in a book but attention focused on the door. When Miss Alderman emerges, she does not stir, allowing her to cross the quadrangle towards the administration block before she follows.

That Miss Alderman has been having an affair with Mr. Ormiston is obvious. His behaviour last week, her familiarity today. Less obvious is the connection between the affair and her suddenly arriving at the Priory School to teach. Cause and effect? Or plan.

The older woman enters the staff wing of the administration building, which is off-limits to students, and the door closes behind her. The door is solid wood, but while it was open she could see the corridor ahead and measures the steps in her head. Putting the book back in her bag, she takes out a sheet of paper about the concert tomorrow—a working alibi in case she is stopped. Then she puts Magnus's key in the door of the administration building, opens the door, and enters.

The corridor is empty. The biggest mistake an intruder makes is looking suspicious, so she walks purposefully down the hall to the wide wooden stairs, up which Miss Alderman's light footsteps are now heading.

She pauses, pretending to read the concert notice long enough for the teacher to reach the top of the stairs, then ascends herself. The stairs continue up to the top floor of the building, but Miss Alderman is now halfway down another corridor, putting her own key in a lock. Her office, presumably. Five doors down on the right hand side.

It was optimistic to have expected her to go straight back to Mr. Ormiston and have a candid conversation about their affair and how she comes to be at the school. Now that she is in her office there is not much to discover and Arcadia is exposed in the open. It is time to beat a retreat.

Heavy footsteps coming down from the upper floor. Headmaster. In addition to the general office side of the building, there must be an entrance to his office from the staff wing. She could probably make it down to the ground floor, but another possibility presents itself. Hastening down the corridor, she looks quickly at the names on the doors. Miss Alderman is using a vacant office. The ones either side are for Mr. Ormiston and Pipe-Major Scott. Bagpiping is an after-school activity so it is unlikely the latter will be returning soon. She quickly opens the door with the master key, slips inside, and shuts it quietly behind her.

The heavy footsteps come down the corridor and pause. There is a single knock and then Miss Alderman's voice: "Enter."

In the adjacent office, she takes an empty glass from the Pipe-Major's table and presses it against the wall so that she can hear every word.

"Why Headmaster," Miss Alderman says. "How delightful to see you again."

"I wish I could say the same," Headmaster replies.

"You're not pleased to see me?"

"It's not that. But I should have been told first."

"I'm afraid that you aren't really in a position to be making any kind of demands, at this point. You completely mishandled the situation with the Stamford boy. You're jeopardising everything."

"I have the situation under control."

"You appear to be the only person who believes that to be the case." Miss Alderman's voice increases in volume and pitch slightly. "We have years of work at stake and we're not going to let you ruin it."

Headmaster retorts in a hoarse whisper: "For heaven's sake will you keep your voice down."

"Listen, Charles," she continues more calmly. "No one has more invested in this than I. But I'm afraid your commitment is starting to be questioned. Can we count on you?"

"Of course you can count on me. That's a ridiculous question. I've been working on this since you were a schoolgirl with pigtails."

There is contempt in the reply. "I never had pigtails, Charles. Now pull yourself together. The parents will be here tomorrow and everything has to be as normal as possible."

"Is that going to be possible if her parents see you?"

"They're *not* going to see me, Charles. Get back to work."

Headmaster does not speak but the door slams and heavy footsteps go back down the corridor and up the stairs.

In the office next door, she puts down the glass thoughtfully. After five minutes Miss Alderman leaves the office also. Arcadia waits for a further five minutes before silently opening the door. She moves through the corridor, down the stairs, and out into the quadrangle.

The afternoon sun just touches the edge of the sandstone buildings; for a moment it looks like the rock is alive, burning with its own fire. But as she stands watching it the sun sinks further and the building is cast into shadow.

8
CONCERT

The next day is Wednesday, the day of the school concert. After finishing a bowl of lukewarm porridge and a sorry-looking banana, she gathers her books and walks across the quadrangle to the classrooms.

The lessons pass in a blur. Outwardly she pays attention and responds as required; inwardly she turns over the data that do not form a complete picture, pieces of a jigsaw puzzle whose size she does not yet know. She considers contacting Magnus once again, but her brother has said to wait. Though they are not exactly close, she knows that she can trust him. For the moment, then, she is on her own.

Except that her parents will be at school this evening. Curious that this fills her not with a sense of reassurance but of responsibility.

"Well hello there, *Arsey!*"

Her reverie is broken by Sebastian, his sidekick Joan Hardy beside him. A slight redness on the boy's nose is all that remains of the previous day's altercation. It is now lunchtime and she is sitting on a bench at the edge of the quadrangle, nibbling distractedly on an apple.

"Hello, Sebastian. I'm afraid I don't really have time for your games today."

Sebastian turns to Joan in mock amazement. "Oh dear, Joan, did you hear what she said? She said she doesn't have time for me today. Oh well, I suppose she doesn't want to hear what has happened to her violin. I try to be a Good Samaritan and look what happens. Serves me right for trying to do something nice."

Joan at last catches on and shakes her head also. "It's a shame, Sebastian. Really a shame."

They turn as if to go and Arcadia sighs. "What about my violin, Sebastian?"

Sebastian turns back, struggling to keep the smile off his face. "Well, I thought it would be hard for you to play in the concert tonight with no violin. Apparently it's disappeared from the music room. Like magic."

"Like magic!" echoes Joan.

She looks more closely at the two. Bluffing is not Sebastian's *forte* and so it is likely that he has indeed stolen her violin. It is half an hour into lunch and Sebastian has little capacity to delay gratification; most probably he has hidden it only recently. Fresh mud on the side of their shoes when there has been no rain suggests the sports field, from which the sound of water sprinklers can still be heard. A bulge in Sebastian's left pocket indicates that

he has borrowed the oversize keys that open the rugby shed—in any case an obvious place for him to hide the violin.

"Sebastian, I would be very grateful if you would put the violin back where it was in the music room," she says.

A look of badly-faked horror spreads across the larger boy's face. "What on earth are you inferring, *Arsey*? That I was somehow involved? I am shocked. Shocked."

"I'm not inferring anything—I'm implying. But perhaps it will save us both time if I just tell you to go back to the rugby shed, get my violin, and return it to the music room."

Sebastian's expression of mock horror is slowly overtaken by a genuine look of surprise.

"How did she—" Joan begins, but Sebastian cuts her off.

"And what makes you think I would do anything to help you?" He is trying to maintain some of his bluster.

She wearies of this. "Because if you don't, then I will arrange for the magazines that you keep in your locker to be posted to your parents. What is 'Big & Bouncy', anyway? I had long assumed it was some kind of soccer magazine, though the ladies in it appear to be a little underdressed for sport. And in case you decide to dispose of the magazines, it will be far harder to erase completely your account on the accompanying website bigandbouncy.com. Perhaps I could email the details to your father?"

It is fascinating to watch Sebastian's facial expressions as surprise transforms into shock and then fear.

"So the violin goes back in the music room," she concludes. "Do we understand each other?"

"Yeah, yeah," Sebastian grumbles.

As they leave, she hears Joan turn to him: "I still don't understand how she knew it was in the rugby shed. Did she follow us?"

"Shut up, Joan," Sebastian says as they head back to the sports field.

She has to strain to hear the rest of the conversation: "So what are you going to say to him?" Joan asks.

"I'll figure something out," replies Sebastian.

That is the last thing she can make out over the background noise of other boys and girls at their lunch break. But as she watches them depart, Sebastian looks up to the administration building and shakes his head.

Following Sebastian's gaze, she sees a man with white hair standing at the window. The man's eyes sweep across the quadrangle. For a moment they lock onto her own. Then Headmaster turns away from the window and is gone.

Evening comes and parents begin to trickle in for the end of year concert. For the school it is an hour and a half designed to showcase the abilities of the students and reassure parents that they are getting their money's worth. For parents it is eighty-five minutes of tedium, broken by five minutes of furtive video-recording for bragging rights and posterity.

The students will perform mostly in groups with a few soloists. In line with tradition, parents are welcomed by the keening sound of the pipe band performing on the quadrangle outside Hall. Pipe-Major Scott is enthusiastically leading the boys, resplendent in their kilts. She suspects that this particular tradition was created to avoid having to listen to the bagpipes being played indoors.

She and the other performers watch the pipe band through the windows of the music room adjacent to Hall. Her parents arrive, but the students are to stay backstage until after the performance is finished and a buffet dinner is served. Beside her, Henry is looking out the window also, absentmindedly fingering the keys on his oboe. Her own violin is safely in its case nearby.

"They will be late, but they will be here," she says.

"We'll see."

"All right boys and girls," says Mrs. Norman-Neruda, the Deputy Director of Music. "Your parents are coming into Hall shortly and I want no disappointed faces. Can I have the woodwind ensemble ready to go, please? The rest of you know your order. If you don't, then this is Miss Alderman who has the list and will be helping out backstage tonight."

Henry moves over to join the woodwinds. As Mrs. Norman-Neruda does some final tuning, Miss Alderman moves through the room ensuring that the other students are prepared.

"You're playing Mendelssohn tonight, Arcadia?" the teacher says when she reaches her. "I look forward to it."

"Thank you," she replies. "But won't you be sitting in the audience? You'll get a much better view."

"That's sweet of you to say. But Headmaster has asked me to stay back here and keep an eye on you lot."

"Ah well," she says. "At least you'll have a chance to meet some of the parents over the buffet dinner afterwards. Mine are here tonight — I would be pleased to introduce you to them."

Miss Alderman hesitates for a second. "Why isn't that kind. But I fear that I have a personal commitment this evening. Another time."

"Of course, Miss," she says graciously. What did Headmaster fear would happen if Miss Alderman and her parents saw each other?

A monitor in the music room shows the view from the back of Hall. The pipe band has concluded its performance and most of the parents are now seated. The students crowd around the monitor to watch.

A round of applause greets Headmaster as he goes up on stage to welcome the parents.

"Greetings, greetings!" he declaims. "Tonight is a very special night at the Priory School. Our annual concert is an opportunity to celebrate the musical accomplishments of all our students. As you know, this school believes that greatness comes in many forms. The role of the school is to help bring out the best in each and every boy—and girl. I like to think that we help provide a spark that lights a flame—but tonight is also an opportunity for us to meet the people who really deserve the credit: you, the parents, whose own talents and support are reflected in the achievements of your sons and daughters."

He leads them in a self-congratulatory round of applause. Then he briefly frowns at something at the back of Hall. It is not visible on the monitor at first, but then two parents can be seen squeezing themselves into a pair of empty seats. The woman is in a designer dress and carrying an expensive handbag. Even without a microphone it is clear that she is scolding the man who accompanies her. Arcadia smiles. At least they didn't miss Henry's performance.

"And now," Headmaster says, "on with the show!" To another round of applause he takes his seat in the front row as Mrs. Norman-Neruda can be seen shepherding the woodwind ensemble onto stage.

In the music room, she checks the time. It is now 7:07pm. Hers is the third last item. A little less than an hour, but now that Miss Alderman is on duty backstage she needs an excuse.

"Miss Alderman," she says a little breathlessly as she approaches her.

"Yes, Arcadia?"

"I need to go and get rosin for my bow. It must have

fallen out from my case, but I have a spare cake in my room. I can't play without it."

The teacher looks at her suspiciously. "It doesn't seem like you to leave things lying about, Arcadia."

Many liars get caught when they over-elaborate. She simply waits.

"Oh very well then," Miss Alderman says at last. "Go and get your rosin."

"Thank you, Miss."

She leaves through the rear door of the music room and crosses the quadrangle towards the dormitories. Only when she is out of sight from the windows of the music room does she double back towards the administration building. She opens the door to the staff wing with the master key and enters.

It is deserted. On this occasion she has neither the time nor the need for artifice. She ascends two flights of stairs, past the corridor with Miss Alderman's office, to the top floor. There is another locked door, which opens onto a darkened corridor. This in turn takes her to the top of the main steps leading from the general office to where Headmaster's secretary, Miss Bennett, sits and a small waiting area. Beyond that is Headmaster's office.

She closes her eyes to picture the image from the surveillance camera that showed Miss Bennett's desk. Located in the ceiling, it covers the desk with its computer and typewriter, the waiting area, and the stairs that lead up from the general office. But it does not show the corridor she has just come down or the door itself. Pressing herself against the wall behind the desk, she edges towards the door. Keeping her body flush against it, she gently inserts the key. It is unlikely that there is any sort of alarm, but she holds her breath to listen as the key turns in the lock. With a satisfying click the aligned pins rotate and the door swings open wide enough for her to step inside.

The sun has not quite set and there is still enough light to identify *Nineteen Eighty-Four* on the bookshelf. She pulls the book back and opens the hidden door to the secret office. Once inside, the light from the computer monitors is sufficient to confirm that the room has no windows. She closes the door to the main office, checking that there is a release on the inside, and switches on the fluorescent light.

The monitors continue to show a live feed from a hundred points around the school. She is confident that her circuitous path has avoided them, though a thorough investigation might reveal that she did *not* appear on the cameras that she should have if she had in fact gone to the dormitory building. A risk she must take.

In any case, she is not here for the cameras.

The filing cabinets are unlocked. She opens the first drawers and quickly establishes that they contain files on all the boys and girls at the Priory School. Each of the 507 current students has a dossier that covers his or her medical, intellectual, and social development, with a section on disciplinary matters. She skims a few and mentally notes the various metrics being used to measure progress — IQ tests and other cognitive scales, but also tracking scores for emotional intelligence, the ability to deal with adversity, and creativity. As Headmaster intimated, the school's resistance to standardised testing did not mean that it fails to monitor the students closely. Interesting that none of these scores are revealed to the students or their parents. But now is not the time to browse.

The dossiers are organised alphabetically by surname and under "Greentree, Arcadia" she locates her own. It is the same file that Mr. Ormiston referred to last Friday night. In addition to her medical history and grades it includes various notes and comments from teachers. These range from a tirade by Mr. Pratt about her insolence to a testimonial from Mrs. Norman-Neruda on her potential as a musician.

Form teachers, it seems, write short essays on their students every month or so. A recent note from Mr. Ormiston includes the circled phrases she saw during last Friday's interview with her parents: "Arcadia is something of a loner, self-absorbed much of the time with occasional anti-social tendencies. But she has potential. If she can only learn to focus her abilities on something larger than herself, I see great things for this young woman," reads one passage. "She has yet to be tested by life. But I think, when that test comes, she will not be found wanting."

She is about to turn the page when an annotation in green pen catches her eye. It says simply "Add to 2ndary file." Flicking through the rest of the folder she sees several similar notations. The same note has been made at the end of Mr. Pratt's account of her alleged insolence. Another is in the margins of a one paragraph description by Mr. Ormiston of her altercation with Sebastian just the previous day. In all, the file is a reasonably complete history of her time at the Priory School. Except for the reference to another file, it is similar to the files on other students.

So where is this secondary file? A digital clock on the wall shows that the time is now 7:32pm. She has fifteen minutes more in the room at the very most.

The other drawers of the filing cabinets contain nothing more than the dossiers. She checks for hidden compartments without success. The files of past students must be stored elsewhere, or digitised.

Unwilling to give up, she turns to the laptop on the table in the centre of the room. Sitting down at the table, her foot makes a dull clang as it hits an aluminium rubbish bin. She holds both feet against it and the room is silent once more, apart from the hum of the servers and the fan. She presses a key on the laptop and its screen flickers to life. The page displayed is stylised logo of a tree with a password prompt. Why a tree? Something to ponder at a later date.

After pausing for a moment she types "Orwell" but it is incorrect. Her chances of guessing the password are remote. The school protocol requires a mix of letters and numbers, and for passwords to be changed every six months. Many people respond to such challenges by writing down the password somewhere near the computer, but that would be careless and a look around the room is not promising. The keyboard is reasonably well-used — unlike the safe in her parents' room it will not give up its secrets so easily.

Then her foot nudges the rubbish bin once more. There is a rustling of paper. She pushes back the chair and takes out the bin. Inside is only a single printed page, but it is from a draft of a letter that appears to have been written that day. A small "2" in the bottom right corner suggests that it is the second page, but there is no first or third. It has been printed and then amendments made with the same green pen used in the files. It reads:

not understand why you have sent ~~that woman~~ "Miss Alderman" here.

I have explained to you on the telephone that the Stamford boy had always been ~~wary of participating~~ reluctant to participate. He feels that he is "ratting on a friend". But he is now under control. His running away was unfortunate, but the situation is now manageable and he understands the consequences of further disobedience.

As you will recall, we continue to have more success with the Harker boy. ~~If anything, he sometimes relishes his role a little too much for my liking.~~ He is very supportive. Following one of the provocation protocols, the subject responded with violence — a first. I will be writing up the incident in the usual way, but the teacher overreacted and sent her to me. ~~I am a little concerned that she is becoming suspicious of her surroundings.~~ I disciplined her mildly and took the opportunity to assess her lateral and critical thinking skills, which remain prodigious but perhaps have not yet peaked. (The Harker boy was mildly injured but has been compensated. He will recover.)

A fuller assessment will be possible only in the context of the end of year tests, when she will once again be given the expanded versions of all the papers. In addition, we will run the usual medical

The page ends in mid-sentence.

The time is 7:41pm. She needs to leave soon. A quick search does not reveal any more paper. Steal the laptop itself? It would allow more time to break the password but would certainly be noticed. She could go back through the files for "Stamford, Henry" and "Harker, Sebastian" but something else nags at her. Obviously she herself is the "subject", but what does it mean that Sebastian's behaviour is part of a "provocation protocol"? The boy must be a better actor than she has given him credit for.

But there is more. Something to do with the proposed medical tests.

It is 7:44pm. She should leave, but returns to the filing cabinets and takes out her own file once more. Inside the front cover is a medical summary with allergies (none), blood type (AB+), and so on. She pauses. It also lists the contact details and basic medical histories of her parents, correctly showing Mother's allergy to penicillin. And her blood type: O+.

Time stops.

How is it possible that she does not know this? Father's blood type is listed. Also O+.

Could it be a mistake?

The clock shows 7:46pm. She must go. There will be time enough to think.

She closes the file and returns it to the filing cabinet. The excerpt from the letter goes back into the rubbish bin and the light goes off. She exits through the bookshelf door and out of Headmaster's office, sticking to the wall to avoid the camera. Down the darkened corridor to the stairs, she descends and comes out onto the quadrangle. The sun has now set and she sucks cool air into her lungs.

There will be time enough to think.

She walks to the door of the music room. She allows herself one second to get composed and enters.

"Arcadia!" Miss Alderman strides across. "What on earth took you so long—I was about to send out a search party. Arcadia, are you all right?" She is now looking at her with concern.

"I'm fine," she whispers. Then repeats in a normal tone: "I'm fine. I guess I'm a little nervous about performing. I had to go to the bathroom. A couple of times."

Vulnerability works. Miss Alderman's face melts slightly. "Oh you poor thing. Did you find your rosin?"

She produces the rosin that has been in her pocket for the past hour and gives Miss Alderman a weak smile.

"OK," she says. "Well, you'd better get ready. There are two more pieces and then you're on."

The violin under her chin is a part of her body, the bow an extension of her arm. She closes her eyes not against the spotlight but against the world. To lose herself, just for a moment, in the music. Mendelssohn's notes reveal themselves, not as a mathematical series of vibrations but as a kind of poetry. Her body sways gently as the violin sings its song without words.

There will be time enough to think.

It is elementary human biology. There are four basic blood groups: A, B, AB, and O. She knew that her blood type is AB and that this is reasonably uncommon. But the parents of a child whose blood is AB must both be either

A, B, or AB. No one with blood type O can have a child whose blood type is AB.

Accompanying on the piano, she does not need to look at Mrs. Norman-Neruda to know that the teacher has moved from keeping time and tune to joining a performance. The piano is the body and the violin is the soul. Yet it also prevents her losing herself completely, as she lost herself once in her room, in a single note. The day Mother lied to her.

And then it is over. There is applause. Mrs. Norman-Neruda is pleased. The lights come up on the audience and she sees Headmaster clapping with apparent enthusiasm. Further back she sees Mother — her mother dabbing a handkerchief to her eyes while her husband applauds and beams. She offers a slight bow and disappears offstage.

Miss Alderman has been standing by the door to the music room, watching her. As she approaches the teacher turns away, but not before she sees the glistening of stage lights reflected by a tear in her eye also.

The final item for the evening requires all students to be on stage. Her violin is back in its case and she takes her place with the others to sing the patriotic hymn "I Vow to Thee, My Country."

I vow to thee, my country, all earthly things above,
Entire and whole and perfect, the service of my
love…

The words wash over her. It is one of Mother's — does she call her Louisa now? — favourite songs. How could they not tell her. How could she not have deduced it herself long ago.

And there's another country, I've heard of long ago,
Most dear to them that love her, most great to
them that know…

It is now so obvious. So clear. Physical characteristics like Mother's hazel eyes compared to her own grey eyes. Differences in the capacity for observation. The fact that Mother clearly does not prepare — or entirely understand — the codes that are set for her on weekends.

And soul by soul and silently her shining bounds
increase,
And her ways are ways of gentleness, and all her
paths are peace.

The concert concludes. Headmaster invites parents, boys, and girls outside for dinner. "That is all!"

Louisa — Mother enfolds her in an embrace. Her husband pats her on the back.

"What's wrong, Arky?" Mother asks.

"Nothing."

Most of the parents and students are leaving Hall for the buffet. Mother reaches across to nudge a lock of dark hair away from Arcadia's eyes. "You always think you're so good at hiding your feelings. But I can tell that something is upsetting you."

If she focuses on the task at hand then things will make sense. If she can concentrate on the problem, the solution will present itself. She just needs to gather a little more data.

"Really," she says, "I'm fine. But could you please wait for me by the piano on the stage? I need to get my violin."

"Of course, dear."

She returns to the music room, now almost empty. Miss Alderman is about to leave through the rear door but Arcadia stops her. "Miss!" she calls out. "Headmaster asked me to find you. He said he needs to speak with you about something. It sounded important."

"Very well," Miss Alderman says without enthusiasm. "Where is he?"

"Waiting by the piano."

"Thanks. By the way, I thought you played very well today, Arcadia."

"Thank you, Miss Alderman."

She picks up her violin case as the teacher leaves the music room, then follows her out into Hall. It is almost empty now and Miss Alderman is halfway across the stage

to the piano when she sees them and checks her step. But they have also seen her.

"Good God!" Mother exclaims. "What are you doing here?"

Arcadia is not far behind Miss Alderman, who turns her head slightly to look back over her shoulder. There is a hint of fear in her eyes, but also the beginning of a wry smile on her lips.

Miss Alderman addresses her parents. "Why Mr. and Mrs. Greentree, it's a pleasure to see you again. I thought Arcadia did wonderfully tonight, don't you?"

Mother is too puzzled and angry to speak. Father responds for her: "Yes, we were very proud. Tell me, uh, how is it that you come to be at the Priory School?"

"I'm a teacher now," says Miss Alderman evenly. "In fact, today is only my second day. I teach science. A substitute for Mr. Pratt while he is in hospital."

"Oh yes," Father replies. "I heard about that. Nasty accident. They suspect the other driver was drunk but still haven't caught him."

"So you three know each other?" she interjects innocently.

"We do," Miss Alderman says, a touch quickly. "We met some years ago when I was at university. Your parents were very kind to me."

Mother is uncomfortable but Arcadia needs to pry a little deeper. "I see," she says. "Miss Alderman taught a very interesting class yesterday." Father frowns at the mention of her name — perhaps he had forgotten it? "It was about the difference between nature and nurture: how we inherit some things from our parents, while others are developed in response to our environment. The line between the two can be quite blurred, of course. Though not in some areas. Blood type, for example. Blood type can only be inherited according to certain rules."

The colour is draining from Mother's face and she has taken hold of Father's hand in her own. "Arky…" she begins. Then she starts to fall.

Father catches her, easing her onto the piano stool. His face creases with concern. "Louisa, you've got to stay calm." He turns to Arcadia but says nothing for several moments. "Listen," he begins. "My dear, I know that we have a lot to talk about. But your mother has been having episodes of heart palpitations again. She'll be fine, but she cannot cope with any more stress this evening. You'll be home on Friday night and I promise you that we'll talk about anything you want to. Can you wait two days?"

She sees the anxiety in Mother's eyes. "Of course I can."

Father helps her to her feet. "I think I should take her home."

Arcadia takes her other arm. "Come, I'll walk you to the car."

They almost forget Miss Alderman. "Good night, Louisa and Ignatius," she says. "I do hope you feel better soon. And good night, Arcadia. Well done this evening."

Miss Alderman returns to the music room as she and

Father walk Mother outside. Her head rests briefly on Arcadia's shoulder as they walk along the path through the quadrangle, leaving the buffet tables behind.

Above them, the sky has darkened and the first stars are visible. Or perhaps one is a planet.

Mother's steps are a little more confident now and she looks up at the night sky. "You know, Arky, you and Magnus were such blessings to us. Oh difficult and worrying, to be sure. But blessings nonetheless."

They continue walking out to the car park.

"And you have such gifts. Eyes that could spot a needle in its haystack. A mind that could calculate the number of straws of hay themselves. Ignatius and I did what we could. But it's years since we could challenge your mind. All we hoped was that we could help develop your heart. That you would have a sense of justice. That your beautiful, cold brain would be able to love and be loved."

Mother sighs. "I don't know if we did any good. But I like to think that we tried. And I know that you tried also."

"It's time to go home, Louisa," Father says. "Arcadia, there will be time enough to speak on the weekend. All right?"

Time enough. Even her thoughts she owes to them.

"Of course. I hope you feel better." She kisses Mother on the cheek. "Good night—Mother. Good night, Father."

And they are gone.

9
WARNINGS

"How long have you known?"

"Known what? My dear Arcadia, you could be referring to most of the contents of any decent encyclopaedia." On the other end of the line, Magnus pauses for a moment. "But from the strain in your voice and your accelerated breathing I would guess that this is something personal. Was it a blood test?"

"How could you not tell me?"

"Ah, it *was* a blood test. But it was always self-evident, surely? Mother has hazel and Father has brown eyes; you and I have grey. The nose is all wrong, the earlobes detached, and fifteen other characteristics. And yes, it is far simpler to keep calling them Mother and Father. I debated it myself for a minute or two when I first found out. But calling your parents by their first names at age seven raises all sorts of awkward questions."

So Magnus has known since he was seven. Sixteen years

her brother has known and not told her.

"I'm afraid that I couldn't tell you, sister dear. Mother swore me to secrecy—though I knew you would find it out for yourself. Eventually.

"And to answer your next question, I'm afraid that I am indeed AB positive also. We could do a DNA test to be certain, but I doubt that it would surprise anyone who knows us both to find out that you and I are, in fact, biologically related."

It is Thursday morning, the day after the concert. She reassembled her phone to call her brother, who insisted on hanging up and contacting her on what he said was a secure line through their computers. There is a slight delay, but the sound is clear enough to hear the strain that her brother's weight is putting on the chair in his rooms at Cambridge.

"But related to whom?"

"Yes, well legally one has to be eighteen before getting access to one's birth records," Magnus responds. "To be frank, for some years I was not particularly bothered to find out. Mother and Father refused to speak about it and begged me not to dig into the matter. I let matters lie but as you began to gurgle your first words I became curious about the sister who had so unexpectedly landed on our doorstep.

"At the time I had the habit of browsing periodically through certain government databases. I had constructed the online identity of a middle-aged man and every now and then would help certain agencies resolve problems that they confronted. It was simplicity itself to enter into the General Register Office and locate our original birth records."

"And was the mother's name," she says, "Sophia Alderman?"

"Hmm? What a curious thought. No it wasn't. Who, pray tell, is Ms. Alderman? A new teacher? Don't tell me Headmaster has finally decided that women can do more than teach art, music and perhaps French?"

She rebukes herself. Of course it was ridiculous—at the time Magnus was born Miss Alderman could only have been in her early teens. "It was just a thought," is all she says.

"Yes, well, carrying on. The names of the parents on both our birth records are John and Euphemia Hebron. Despite the slightly unusual name—not that you or I should be casting stones in that area—they were both Scottish. He was what they refer to as a 'main street lawyer', which I believe is the polite thing to call a lawyer who doesn't make much money. He had a small practice in Banbury. She was an administrator at a nearby comprehensive school.

"They were both reasonably well educated, with degrees from lower-tier universities, but nothing really to distinguish them as exceptional intellects. What did distinguish them was that Euphemia suffered from severe depression and the family was unable to cope with the responsibilities of child-rearing. This, at least, was the

reason given on the adoption forms that they completed when they put me up for adoption.

"Ignatius and Louisa are, you may have deduced, unable to have children naturally. They had been on a waiting list for some time—the essay they wrote on their reasons for wanting to raise a child is really quite touching."

"What happened to the Hebrons?" she asks. "You were using the past tense to describe them."

"I was getting to that, Arcadia," her brother replies. "Seven years later they had another child: you. Soon after your birth at the John Radcliffe Hospital, however, they died in a car crash. You were only a few weeks old. Fortunately, I suppose, the same officer was put in charge of your case and he contrived to approach Louisa and Ignatius—Mother and Father—about adopting a sibling. They agreed and here you are."

"But did the Hebrons leave anything? Did they at least write a letter?"

"Not that I know of, Arcadia. They don't seem to have been the most reflective sort."

"What about relatives. Have you spoken to them?"

"What would be the point?"

Her brother's apathy is exasperating. "Aren't you even curious to know more about your heritage, where you come from?"

"Arcadia, all we share with the Hebrons is some DNA. If they were alive I can imagine a certain interest in meeting them—much as your own development as a child gave me the opportunity to reflect on certain of my own qualities. But their own parents and siblings get further and further removed to the point where any link would be purely sentimental.

"I concede that a full medical history might one day be of interest. Here I regret to inform you that the late Mrs. Hebron's depression most probably did have a genetic component—though, again, the fact that you and I are predisposed to melancholy is not exactly 'news'.

"So, dear sister, I'm afraid that I appear to be your only biological family. Not terribly reassuring, I imagine. But there you have it."

She digests all this. "What about the surveillance cameras at our house? When I mentioned them to you the other day you nearly destroyed my phone."

"I did nothing of the sort. I merely exercised reasonable precautions, as I always do, to avoid leaving a messy digital trail. But I have made a few inquiries. I hope to know more today or tomorrow."

"Thank you. There's something else. I realise that this might sound paranoid, but I discovered that Headmaster is keeping a secret file on me. He has also recruited students to report on my behaviour. In a fragment of a letter, he describes me as 'the subject' and how one of these students followed a protocol in order to test my reactions. This Sophia Alderman has some connection also—and when I staged a meeting between her and our parents, it was clear that they had met before."

"Arcadia, to anyone else it might sound paranoid, but I am presently sitting in a college bedroom that I have used wire mesh to convert into a Faraday cage as protection against electronic surveillance. To your question, Mr. Milton's approach to education was always a little eccentric. Many of the cameras at school were installed while I was still a yearling. Does he still watch them directly himself? One wonders how he finds hours in the day.

"Let me look into that also. Infuriatingly, I have to leave college on an errand, so I'll text you later in the day. Which reminds me: you can leave your phone in one piece. I don't know what you were thinking that would achieve — you aren't exactly hard to find. Cheerio."

Later that morning she has English with Mr. Ormiston. They finish their discussion of Edgar Allen Poe just as the bell rings to indicate the start of lunch.

"I thought that you might enjoy Poe, Miss Greentree," Mr. Ormiston says, walking over as she is putting her books away. "I always liked Poe's stories about C. Auguste Dupin myself."

"His methods are certainly interesting," she replies absently.

Mr. Ormiston looks to see that the other students have left the classroom, then says more quietly: "Arcadia, is everything all right? You haven't seemed yourself for the past few of days."

Is she that transparent?

"I know that you're highly strung at the best of times," Mr. Ormiston continues, "but violence at school, daydreaming in class… Is there anything I need to know?"

Is there anything he does not already know? Given the way in which Miss Alderman has manipulated him, however, it is possible that he is not aware of the machinations underway. How might she test for this? Clearly Miss Alderman and Headmaster must know about her parentage. Does Mr. Ormiston?

A risk, but one worth taking. It should appear spontaneous. "I just found out that I was adopted," she blurts.

Mr. Ormiston appears lost for words. He takes half a step forward, perhaps considering a hug or some other gesture, then stops. "Oh, Arcadia," is all he says. "Oh dear. That must be— that must be a shocking thing to discover. I'm so sorry." He is not a good enough actor to be faking his surprise and concern, which is therefore genuine. "Did you just find out?"

"Yes," she replies. "My parents confirmed it last night."

"Look, Arcadia, you know the school has counsellors for this sort of thing. But my door is always open to you. How are you feeling about all this at the moment?"

"It was a bit of a shock," she says truthfully. "But I'll be OK."

"If there's anything I can help with, please let me know."

"Thank you, Mr. Ormiston."

She is about to leave when Miss Alderman herself enters. "Good day, Arcadia," the substitute teacher says coolly. "What a nice coincidence meeting your parents like that last night. I did catch up with Headmaster, by the way. How strange, though: he didn't recall asking you to fetch me."

"I'm sorry," she says. "I must have made a mistake."

"Perhaps you did." Turning to Mr. Ormiston: "William, I wondered if you might like to join me for lunch?"

"Why thank you, Miss Alderman," Mr. Ormiston looks down at his feet. There has been some kind of cooling between them also; perhaps he is thinking of his wife. "Unfortunately I've got a lot of marking to do today. The students have submitted their essays on Poe. Arcadia and I were just discussing it."

"We were," she adds, watching Miss Alderman closely. "One of them, 'The Purloined Letter', is about a woman who possesses certain information that she seeks to conceal. Yet she unwittingly puts it in the hands of a person who can use it to their advantage."

If Miss Alderman is in the slightest perturbed, she does not reveal it. She is by far the better actor of the two teachers. "I think I recall the story," she says, meeting Arcadia's gaze. "Isn't it the one in which the thief thinks he is so cunning by hiding it in plain sight? The woman's agent finds the letter, however, replacing it with a fake. So in the end, it is the woman who has the thief in her power."

Touché. Arcadia inclines her head to acknowledge the minor victory. All she says is: "Miss Alderman, Mr. Ormiston, if I may be excused?"

"Of course, Arcadia," says Mr. Ormiston. "And remember what I said. Please feel free to call on me."

"Thank you, sir."

She leaves, but does not go far. The classroom is on the ground floor and on one side its open windows face a small copse of trees. It is a plausible place for a girl to sit and read with her back to the wall, underneath a window. Magnus and so many others assume that surveillance must depend on high technology. Yet the origin of the term 'eavesdropping' is precisely that one can learn a lot from loitering under the eaves of a building and listening. So it is that she overhears the ongoing conversation between Mr. Ormiston and Miss Alderman.

"I'm sorry, Sophia," Mr. Ormiston is saying. "I'm really not comfortable continuing like this."

"Not *comfortable*?" Miss Alderman sounds unimpressed. "You seemed to enjoy all the comfort you could get from me on Monday night."

"That was a mistake. It won't happen again." He is trying to end the conversation. "Look, I've helped you as much as I can. I got you this job. But from now on, we just have to be colleagues. Can we try that, please?"

There is a pause. Is she thinking? Calculating. "I guess so," she says at last. Then, a little too innocently: "What were you and the Greentree girl talking about? It didn't look like you were discussing Poe."

"Oh she's just had a bad week," Mr. Ormiston replies.

"Anything important?" She is fishing.

"Some personal matters. She's got a lot of thinking to do — and some long conversations to have at home, that's all. But she'll be fine."

"I hope so," Miss Alderman says.

"Me too. Anyway, as I said, I have these papers to grade. 'Bye, Sophia."

"Goodbye, William."

Mr. Ormiston leaves the classroom first, but Miss Alderman stays. The sound of a clasp opening — her handbag. The gentle tap of a number being dialled on a touch phone. There is no way to hear the other party, but most of her side of the conversation is clear.

"I have an update. She suspects something. The stunt last night was only the beginning. I followed them to the car and the talk was mostly sentimental, but it seems like they're planning a big heart-to-heart this weekend."

She did not notice the teacher's presence at the car park. Another skill to add to her résumé.

"There's something else. She intimated that she knows something about my role. Ormiston remains oblivious, of course. But as you've said before, the girl is very observant."

There is another pause.

"No, I can't predict what they might do. ... You will go and see them yourself? Very well. 'Bye."

Monsieur Dupin was also skilled, lulling his adversary into a false sense of security and then diverting their attention with a distraction. It might not have been a gunshot on the streets of Paris and she might not have the purloined letter in her hand, but she is at last starting to build a picture of her adversaries.

Though the school prohibits the use of mobile phones, she keeps hers in her pocket on silent mode through the day. Yet it is only after dinner when a vibration finally indicates the arrival of a text from Magnus. She is back in her dormitory room when she reads the message:

> Arcadia, do let me know if you'll come up this weekend, watch the boat races and stay for dinner? Out of interest, for once you were right; our Mother and Father did brag to me about your concert. "Parents" as they say! Magnus.

Her brother always writes text messages in full sentences, but the incorrect use of a semi-colon and the ironic application of an exclamation point are clear

indications of a second message. Taking each word after a punctuation mark reveals:

Do watch out for our "parents". Magnus

Well this is unhelpfully ambiguous. "Watch out" implying that she should guard against some danger to them — or that they are a potential source of danger themselves? She quickly types a response using the same simple code to let her brother know that the person Miss Alderman phoned was going to see them:

Thanks Magnus. She did enjoy concert. Called earlier but you were out — someone I know? Going to be a busy weekend, to be sure. See you soon. ("Parents" indeed!) Arcadia.

She does not want to alarm her parents and in any case will be seeing them herself tomorrow night. At that point some more pieces of the puzzle may reveal themselves. She is about to return to her Latin when the insistent buzzing of her phone gets her attention once more. Not a text, it is Magnus calling her directly.

"Why Magnus," she begins. "What an unexpected —"

He cuts her off in a tone of urgency that she has never heard from her corpulent brother. "Arcadia, I'm afraid that our parents are in grave danger. I have tried calling the house but the phone is disconnected. Their mobiles are off or disabled. I have phoned the police and persuaded them to look in, but they may take some time to reach the house."

She sees the danger at once. Potential revelation of whatever plot is underway. Concerns escalated from Headmaster to Miss Alderman to the unknown party whom she called earlier in the day. A promised visit. But could physical violence really be a possibility?

She is already putting on her shoes with one hand, holding her phone with the other. "I'm going home myself," she says. "It's only a short drive from school. I can slip out and get a taxi."

"Arcadia, be careful. Even I have had difficulty investigating this. Whoever is involved knows how to cover their tracks—and such people generally dislike having those tracks revealed."

"I understand. I'll phone you from home."

She hangs up, puts the phone in her pocket, and heads out into the night air. Getting a taxi at this time will not be simple, but first she has to get out of the school grounds without being stopped. The staff parking lot is the best option. Secured by a gate her master key should open, it has its own exit onto the adjacent street.

"Miss Greentree?"

She has not gone ten yards from the dormitory when she hears her name. It is Mr. Ormiston, also walking towards the parking lot. The time is a little after 8pm. There must

have been a staff meeting. It is impractical to run. None of the most plausible lies would be of much assistance. For the second time today, she settles on the truth.

"Mr. Ormiston, I fear something terrible has happened at home. My brother has phoned the police, but we can't get through to our parents. I was about to see if I could go there myself. Could you help me get a taxi?"

Her teacher looks at her closely. School rules are fairly clear on when students are allowed off campus, and there are protocols to follow when seeking exceptions. Forms to fill in.

"No," Mr. Ormiston says after a moment's hesitation. "I'll drive you myself. Come on."

They quicken their step towards the staff car park. Mr. Ormiston opens the gate and they climb into his Jaguar. The engine purrs and then roars as they leave the school grounds.

"You had a staff meeting?" she asks.

Mr. Ormiston nods, his attention on the road.

"Were Headmaster and Miss Alderman there?"

Mr. Ormiston turns his head for a second. "Yes, why?"

"Just curious."

The car screeches to a halt.

"Arcadia," Mr. Ormiston begins. "I'm breaking about fifteen rules in our code of conduct by doing this. The least you can do is tell me the truth."

A reasonable request, in the circumstances. "Fair enough," she says. "There is some connection between

Miss Alderman and my parents, something to do with my adoption. I don't know the full details yet, but I'm worried that my parents could be in danger."

"Danger? From whom?"

"I really don't know."

The car moves again. "And what is Headmaster's connection to all this?"

"That I'm not sure about either. He and Miss Alderman know each other from some time in the past. Yet he was surprised when you arranged for her to teach at the school."

From his reaction, this confirms something that Mr. Ormiston has suspected. "All right, we're on the main road. You'll need to give me directions from here."

She does so, using her phone at the same time to try her parents' house and their mobile numbers. There is no answer.

"Please hurry," she says.

Mr. Ormiston nudges the car past the speed limit, gliding along the country road. Above them, the full moon shines down from a cloudless sky.

10
SCARLET

She walks towards the house, dimly aware of a voice behind calling for her to wait. Her teacher has locked the Jaguar and is hastening to catch up with her.

Moonlight illuminates the quiet street. There are no people, few cars. Her parents' vehicle is in the driveway. Outside the house no other car is parked, but on the footpath outside the house is a single cigarette butt. Lucky Strike. Smoked in the past few hours, flattened into the concrete.

The low front gate is open, but that is not unusual. Her parents were trusting types. Are. Her parents are trusting types.

The path to the front door is also concrete, but the doormat has traces of mud. Five lines of diminishing thickness. She sniffs the mud and takes a tiny piece of it in her fingers. Clayey, not from their garden.

The lights are on. The door is locked. The bell is to the

right. It is a cool night, but not cold enough for gloves. Unlikely but possible that the white button will reveal a fingerprint. She knocks once, twice. There is no sound.

She has a key and uses it. Opens the door.

"Hello!"

Silence.

She looks before entering. Footprints on the carpet in the foyer are a confused mix, but flecks of the same mud identify a series of short steps next to the empty hat stand. With each step the mud is less visible, but two long strides can be seen going down the hallway, along with her parents' smaller footsteps.

Above the hallway is the light fitting. Even knowing what she is looking for, it is difficult to spot the tiny camera. But it is still there, silently transmitting an image of everyone who comes and goes from the house. But who is watching?

Keeping clear of the footprints, she moves down the hallway towards the living room. Behind her she hears Mr. Ormiston entering the house.

"Please don't touch anything," she calls. Her voice sounds hoarse.

In addition to the mud there are four scarlet drops on the hallway carpet. But it is impossible to tell if they fell on the way down to the living room. Or on the way back.

With a growing sense of dread she reaches the living room. It is there that she sees the bodies. Mother and Father, lifeless. They are on the ground next to the sofa.

Their fingers just touching.

Stabbed. A sharp knife. Father once, deep in the chest. Mother on her arms and in the right side of the throat. He was taken by surprise; she fought back. His eyes are open, unblinking at the ceiling. Hers are shut.

There is so much scarlet. So much blood.

She should run and embrace their bodies, but this might interfere with the evidence. She should cry, but this would cloud her vision.

The window next to the back door has been smashed from the outside and the door is ajar. Shards of glass litter the floor, a few pieces lie on top of the blood-spattered carpet like so many irregular rubies.

On the coffee table, three feet from the bodies, there are two faint circles. Whisky. And a smaller circle for Mother's glass of water.

"Dear God!" It is Mr. Ormiston's voice as he enters the living room. "What happened here?"

The teacher has taken out his phone and dials three digits. "Magnus has already called the police," she says softly.

She closes her eyes, shutting out the world. Only the facts matter now, not feelings. The observable evidence. And she puts herself into the other's shoes to reconstruct the crime:

I park away from their house to avoid suspicion, walking the last hundred yards while having a cigarette. To prepare.

One last drag on the cigarette and I drop it to the ground, extinguishing it underfoot.

At the doorstep I wipe the mud from my boots. I wore these boots earlier today while walking on the clayey soil of the countryside, possibly a farm. I am fastidious. But I am also nervous. I cannot clean them completely. Traces of mud remain and are tracked onto the carpet.

My visit is unexpected. Otherwise Louisa would have made tea, laid the table, produced biscuits. Yet they do not turn me away. Instead they invite me in, hanging my jacket on the hat stand.

Ignatius pours two glasses of whisky. She has a glass of water. We chat. Reminisce. We are old friends.

It is not certain that I will kill them. If it were, I would strike immediately. Instead we talk. I ask them to do something, to agree to something. But they refuse. And soon it becomes clear how this must end.

The knife is light in my hand. It is an extension of my hand. An extension of my will. Concealing it behind my back, I continue to smile and gesture with my right hand while the left prepares the blade.

They suspect nothing, of course. Their dulled senses do not perceive that even I struggle to keep my voice at its normal pitch, to prevent beads of sweat forming on my brow. All is outwardly calm, all normal. All illusion.

Amiably, I smile. I laugh. Yes, that is indeed an interesting story. All the while imagining it done. For it must be done.

And then I strike.

First Ignatius, who is caught unawares. The blade goes under his ribs and into his heart. He dies quickly.

She fights back, the knife cutting her arms. But a blow to the neck fells her.

The two bodies are on the ground. I am flustered. I had a plan, but now I am improvising.

I open the back door and smash the window with... with my shoe, to give the appearance of a break-in. I take the glasses, wash them, and put them away.

But I am careless. The mud from my shoes. The unwiped table. Drops of blood land in the hallway. I take my coat and return to the car. It has not gone exactly according to plan, but the street is quiet. Their bodies will not be found at least until tomorrow, when Ignatius is missed at work or when their daughter comes back from school for the weekend.

I return to the car and drive away under a moonlit sky.

It is done.

She opens her eyes once more to look at the bodies that were her parents. Father looks at peace, his face relaxed. Mother's is frozen in the struggle of her last minutes, her eyes glassy with tears.

But her eyes are open.

"She's not dead," Arcadia whispers. Then she hears her own voice shouting: "Call an ambulance!"

Crouching by Mother, she sees that the blood is seeping from a vein in the side of her neck, not spurting from an artery. A lot of blood has been lost, but there is a faint pulse and the shallowest of breaths. She puts her hand on the wound to staunch the bleeding until Mr. Ormiston arrives with a kitchen towel. An ambulance is on its way. In her delirium Mother's eyes occasionally meet her own, focusing and unfocusing on her face. Lips twitch as if to speak but no sound comes out.

The police arrive first, those summoned by Magnus: Constable Lestrange once again, accompanied by a senior officer—the inspector who came to the Priory School with her on Monday. She hears Mr. Ormiston give them a quick summary and they rush to get the medical kit from their van. The ambulance is coming.

The dressing on her wounds has stopped the flow of blood by the time the paramedics arrive. They clear her airways and put her on oxygen, giving her an injection for what must be unbearable pain. The lines on her face smooth slightly.

Mother is placed on a stretcher trolley. One of the paramedics explains that they must take her to hospital as quickly as possible for a transfusion.

"She's O positive," she tells them. "I'm sorry that I can't give her a transfusion—I'm AB positive."

"That's OK, missy," one replies. "We'll give her some plasma in the ambulance and start the transfusion at the hospital. They've got plenty of O positive there. But we need to leave right now. Is there someone who can take you to the hospital?"

"I'll take her," says Mr. Ormiston.

She walks alongside the trolley as they load Mother into the ambulance. "I'll be there soon," she whispers, knowing that she probably cannot hear her.

The doors shut and the ambulance heads off at speed, lighting up the street with rotating blue beams.

"Is there anything you need to get before we go to the hospital?" Mr. Ormiston asks her.

She forces herself to focus, to concentrate. Magnus is coming and they must work together. "Yes," she says, "just give me a minute."

She goes back inside and is about to head upstairs when the two police officers come down the hallway. They do not notice her. Or anything else, it seems.

"So you see, Lestrange," the older inspector is saying, "we have a case here of breaking and entering through the rear door. The victims probably came home, surprised the thief who attacked them with his knife. Having planned on burglary rather than murder, he then exits through the back door. A relatively simple case, but difficult unless the lady pulls through and is able to give us a description."

"I see, Inspector Bradstreet," Constable Lestrange nods.

"See what?" she says, unable and unwilling to disguise her contempt. "Congratulations, Inspector, you have correctly identified the suspect as male. On every other count, of course, you could not be more wrong."

"Young lady," replies Bradstreet. "I understand that you are probably in shock and so will overlook any rudeness on your part. But I advise you to let us do our job."

"I would be happy to do so if you displayed the slightest competence in it."

"Now look here—" Bradstreet begins, but Lestrange cuts him off.

"Ah sir, as you say, the lass is in shock. But perhaps we might hear what she has to say. It could be, er, therapeutic." He turns to her. "So then, Miss Greentree, what do you see?"

"Well, that you should be looking for a left-handed man who is around six feet tall. He was in the countryside earlier today, smokes Lucky Strike cigarettes, and is well-educated—possibly a medical doctor. He is a person who knew my parents reasonably well in the past, but has since fallen out of touch. He is fastidious in his habits and yet excitable, nervous even. Oh, and he entered and left through the front door, not the rear."

Bradstreet is beginning to turn purple again. "And just how do you claim to have deduced all that?"

She should go to the hospital, but there is a slim chance that if she pushes these officers in the right direction they will have a better chance of finding the man who attacked her parents.

"That he is left-handed is clear from the wounds, which are mainly on the right sides of the bodies. His height and his country visit can be seen in the mud on the doormat and the length of stride down the hall. A Lucky Strike cigarette was extinguished on the street before he came in, you can find it there still. His education can be inferred from his precise knowledge of human anatomy. He must have known my parents because they invited him in for a glass of whisky even though he had not called ahead — if he had, then Mother would have laid the table — at least for tea and cake. You will recall, Constable, her unfailing hospitality when you were here."

Despite himself, Lestrange smiles.

"Your man is also fastidious but excitable: he wiped his foot five times on the doormat. And yet he also made mistakes: the mud from his shoes, the unwiped table, drops of blood in the hallway. As for your theory of entry and exit, he does indeed want us to think that he smashed his way in the back door. You may recall, however, that someone managed to break in that door two days ago without smashing the window. In any event, in this case when the window was smashed some pieces landed on top of blood drops on the carpet. Unless painstakingly moved, the shards of glass landed on the floor after the blood was already spilled."

"That's incredible," she hears Lestrange say under his breath.

"Yes, well, thank you, Miss Greentree, for your little theories," says Inspector Bradstreet. "We shall of course consider them closely. But for the moment I suggest that you head to the hospital. Your teacher is driving you, correct?"

"Correct," she replies.

"Then get whatever it is you came inside to get and go to the hospital. Your mother needs you now."

"Yes, Inspector Bradstreet."

She goes upstairs to her parents' bedroom. She knows that she should simply confide in the police, but their efforts to date have not inspired much confidence. It is also possible that she would be leading them on a wild goose chase. She opens Mother's underwear drawer and takes out the Chinese box that is hidden behind the false back. A red stain on the wood draws her attention until she realises that her left hand is still damp with Mother's blood.

She washes her hands in the en suite and takes the box to her room. The box and a change of clothes go into a backpack and she returns downstairs. Until she has conferred with Magnus, she resolves not to say anything further to the police — about the cameras, Miss Alderman, or Headmaster. She steps outside to where Mr. Ormiston is waiting. They get back in the car and drive towards the hospital, the backpack on her lap.

She phones Magnus. Her brother listens to the terse update. "I'll come at once," is all he says. "See you at the hospital."

They drive in silence for a while.

"How did you know?" Mr. Ormiston asks.

"Know what?"

"You said at school that you feared something terrible

had happened. How?"

"I didn't. It was my brother who told me." How could she not have seen it herself?

"So, how did he know?"

She considers this. "My brother is well-connected, but he is also adept at drawing connections. Far better than I. He saw, when I did not, that tugging at this web could lead to disastrous consequences."

"What 'web'?"

"Whatever it is that connects Headmaster, Miss Alderman, and the person to whom she spoke earlier today."

"You think Sophia is connected to what happened at your house?"

"I'm not sure. But when she said that my parents and I were going to have a long discussion this weekend, the person on the other end of the phone decided to go and see them."

"Arcadia, we have to tell the police this."

"Not yet. Let me speak with Magnus first."

"You said he's coming from Cambridge? That could take more than an hour."

"Magnus will find a way."

They arrive at the hospital, pulling into the car park as a helicopter passes overhead and lands on the roof. It pauses for only a minute and then takes off once more, the beating of its blades fading as it disappears back into the night sky.

"What on earth is a military helicopter doing here?" Mr. Ormiston muses to himself, craning his neck to watch it depart.

"It's probably my brother."

They enter the intensive care unit just as Magnus walks in, slightly unsteady, dark hair askew. A raised hand stops her question. "I shall be fine," he says. "I called in a favour to get here quickly, but will not be returning to Cambridge by helicopter. Now, how is Mother?"

A nurse explains that Mother is in surgery and that they cannot see her yet. They are taken to a waiting room where a doctor briefs them.

"So there is good news and bad news," the doctor says. "The good news is that the main wound was clean and didn't damage the carotid artery, which supplies blood to the brain. We are almost finished patching up her throat. The bad news is that she has lost a great deal of blood. We're giving her a transfusion, but in cases of massive blood loss the brain may not get enough oxygen and the patient can fall into a coma—a kind of deep sleep."

"We know what a coma is," Arcadia says testily. "Will she wake up? And what are the chances of permanent loss of brain function?"

The doctor looks at her, her brother, and Mr. Ormiston, reassessing her communication strategy. "It's too soon to say. There was significant injury to both the external and internal jugular veins as well as her trachea. Even if she wakes up, we don't know what kind of brain damage she might have suffered. There is also a high likelihood of nerve damage, meaning that she could be partially or totally paralysed."

"Thank you, Dr. Jackson," Magnus says. "When are you likely to make another assessment?"

The doctor frowns, realising that she forgot to introduce herself—but also forgetting that her name is on the ID card at her waist. "I'll come back to you in about an hour. You can stay here if you like."

Dr. Jackson returns to the ICU, leaving the three of them in the waiting room. It is now 11pm.

"It's good to see you again, Magnus." Mr. Ormiston is trying to make small talk. "A shame about the circumstances, of course."

"I forget myself," says her brother. "A pleasure to see you also, Mr. Ormiston. And do give my best wishes to Mrs. Ormiston—you are making the right decision."

Mr. Ormiston opens his mouth to ask something, but Magnus moves seamlessly on. "Now, Arcadia," he says, "tell me about these cameras."

"The cameras themselves are approximately a quarter inch in diameter and an inch and a half long," She pictures the cameras in her mind's eye, "with a thin cord connecting them to what appears to be a power source and transmitting device. I found four in the house, but have not conducted a complete search. There could be more."

"Matchstick cameras," says Magnus. "Expensive, but not hard to purchase in the open market. You're sure that the attached unit did not have a recording capacity? A shame, but it means that someone may be in possession of a video of the attack on our parents. Such devices can transmit up to a hundred yards, so the recording device could be inside the house or nearby.

"More interesting is the question of who planted it. From what you have said and the reports that the police have filed thus far, the break-in on Tuesday and today's events look very different. It is highly likely that these were two separate actors—and that the man who murdered Father and so gravely injured Mother does not know that there is a recording."

Mr. Ormiston has been restraining himself but is unable to do so any longer. "I don't understand how you two can remain so calm. You lost your father. Your mother is in a coma. Aren't you even in the least bit affected by this?"

They both look at him. "Of course we are 'affected'," says Magnus at last. "But breaking down in tears won't help her and we don't have time to cycle through the stages of grief. Or, if it will make *you* feel better, I can do so quickly: This can't be—it's not fair! Why don't you take me instead, God? I'm so sad. But I have to get on with my life."

"Magnus," Arcadia says gently. "He's just trying to help."

"Of course he is." Magnus turns to Mr. Ormiston: "I

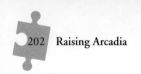

do apologise. But if you would like to help then perhaps you can tell us more about the woman known as Sophia Alderman?"

Mr. Ormiston weighs something and then decides to speak. "Very well. I met her about a year ago at a teachers' conference. She's a part-time science instructor. She had come out of a messy divorce. One thing led to another and—" he breaks eye contact and looks at the ground.

"Do part-time instructors typically get invited to these 'teachers' conferences'?" Magnus asks.

"Sometimes. Well, not usually. No."

"At what point did she ask you to do something for her?"

Mr. Ormiston's eyes widen. "We—we started an affair. At first it was—it was a fling, we would meet up occasionally. I'm not proud of what I did. And I'm only telling you in case there is a chance it will help you find out what happened to your parents. But one night she—she took some photographs of me. In a compromising situation. Then earlier this week she threatened me. She said she wanted a part-time position at the Priory School. If I didn't arrange it, she said she would send the photographs to my wife. I told her there were no positions available for a science teacher. Then when Mr. Pratt had an accident—oh, dear God…"

"With Mr. Pratt indisposed and Miss Alderman conveniently available, you thought it couldn't hurt to recommend her for the position." Magnus finishes the account for Mr. Ormiston, whose head is now in his hands. "As for Mr. Pratt's accident—a hit-and-run with a motor vehicle, or something of the sort?—I understand your inference that it might have been no accident. But have you or anyone else actually seen him in hospital? Is it possible that he has other reasons for absenting himself from the school for several weeks, and allowing Miss Alderman to take his place?"

A minute passes in silence.

"Miss Alderman does have a background in science," Arcadia observes. "Possibly including some graduate study—though she said that she made a choice that was incompatible with completing it. She also has some proficiency in acting, perhaps including professional work after her university days."

"Interesting," Magnus muses. "She certainly deploys her acting skills to some effect. For it turns out that there is no Sophia Alderman. Or rather, there are several—but none that correspond to the person presently teaching science at the Priory School. After you mentioned her in the context of our biological parents I did some basic background checks. Whatever this woman's name is, she has done impressive work in creating a false identity under the name 'Sophia Alderman'. The only way I discovered the artifice was that her records, though complete, do not appear in the backups of databases that are more than a year old. That broadly corresponds to the timeline of what Mr. Ormiston here has described. The scenario of entrapment in this manner is what is known among spies,

I believe, as a 'honeypot'."

Mr. Ormiston stands up. "I have to phone my wife. Tell her where I am."

Yes, or she will assume you are with that woman again. But Arcadia simply nods as her teacher steps out into the corridor to make his call.

"There's a further dimension to all of this," she says to her brother. "Do you recall how Mother would set codes for us to solve on Saturday mornings?"

"Of course." For the first time that day, Magnus's face creases into a smile. "It began as a game that we would play. She set a puzzle for me to win a treat or find some money. After you turned five, she would ask me to include you in solving the codes. That slowed things down, of course, but I believe she wanted to foster some kind of sibling bond between us. I gather she now uses this to send you on the occasional shopping errand."

"Did you ever wonder where she got the puzzles from?"

The smile fades. "She would joke that it was her little secret." Magnus says. "It was evident that she was not making them up herself. I assumed that she had purchased a book of puzzles or periodically browsed the Internet for ideas about codes." The beginnings of a frown appear on his forehead. "But you now suspect that these puzzles were delivered to her? To what end?"

"I'm not sure. But I found this box in her dresser." She produces the Chinese box from her backpack and enters the combination zero-one-six. She opens the box to reveal the stack of envelopes. "Each envelope is sealed, with a post-it note indicating a future Saturday. This box contains envelopes for the rest of term."

She takes out the envelope on top, marked for Saturday, the day after tomorrow. "I steamed this one open to check what was inside. It's unlike any of the earlier codes." The glue has resealed so she rips the envelope open to reveal the message within:

"Interesting," says her brother. "A substitution cipher, clearly. Impractical to solve without more text, unless — oh, I see it was for *you*, wasn't it Arcadia? So 'Nicely done, Arcadia. You are nearly ready.' Very interesting. But I can't really see Mother coming up with that herself."

"I agree," she says. "And why are the envelopes sealed? Mother needed to know the answer. How else would she have known where to hide the reward?"

"The solution must have been explained to her somehow. Perhaps there is a separate stack of answers. Perhaps she received a message each week, timed to coincide with the note."

"But from whom?"

"That, dear sister," Magnus says, "is the all-important

question. Father's death and the attempt on Mother's life are clearly connected with the unravelling of efforts to monitor and shape your development. These codes now look to be part of that monitoring. The fact that in this message, dated two days hence, you are congratulated for solving something on your own gives me a deep sense of unease. Was it mere chance that you happened upon this envelope ahead of time?"

"Yes," she replies. "It was reasonably well hidden. But this would make no sense as a code if Mother put it out for me. And surely she would see the strangeness of it also?"

"Unless whoever provided the code assumed that she would not be in a position to leave the code out this Saturday morning." Magnus sits back in the waiting room chair.

"But then, why are there nine more envelopes?" She tears open the envelope for the following Saturday and takes out the note inside. It is blank. Holds it to the light but there is no invisible ink. She opens envelopes for the successive Saturdays. All contain blank sheets that she drops on the floor.

"Curiouser and curiouser," says Magnus.

"What does it mean?" she asks, mostly to herself.

"Why, dear sister, for perhaps the third time in my life I have no idea."

She and Magnus are sitting in silence when Dr. Jackson returns to the waiting room. "You can see your mother now. She's still in a coma, but she's stable."

They walk behind her into the corridor, where Mr. Ormiston is just finishing his phone call. He follows them, but waits at the door when they enter Mother's room.

The blood has been cleaned from her face and a hospital gown has replaced her clothes. Bandages cover most of her neck and arms; tubes connect her to the various machines that now help her heart to beat and her lungs to breathe. An electrocardiogram tracks the uncertain rhythm of her life.

"There are mixed views on whether comatose patients can actually hear and understand people around them," Dr. Jackson says. "We haven't yet attempted a full assessment as she's still under anaesthetic. But there's good evidence that speaking positively to a loved one can have a beneficial effect. I'll leave you with her for a few minutes."

She gives them a professional smile and walks off to check on other patients. Son and daughter approach either side of the bed in which Mother lies — sleeping, and yet more than sleeping. Arcadia reaches out to touch her hand, gently lifting it to hold it in her own. She looks across the bed at her brother, to find that Magnus has done the same.

11
ENDINGS

They sleep for a few hours on the chairs in the waiting room. As day begins to break, Dr. Jackson advises them to go home and get some proper rest. Mother's condition remains stable and is unlikely to change in the next few hours.

Mr. Ormiston says that they are welcome to stay at his house, but Magnus needs to return to Cambridge and takes a taxi to the train station. He will be back at the hospital by early afternoon. For her part, she asks for one more favour from her teacher.

As they are driving back towards home, she receives a call from her Aunt Jean and Uncle Arthur. Magnus informed them last night of Father's death; they are now making arrangements to come up from their farm in Surrey and will be organising a funeral service on Monday, three days from now.

After she hangs up, Mr. Ormiston turns from the road

to look at her: "You really have to tell the police what you know."

"I understand that," she says. "But I need to check a couple of things first."

"If you don't inform them, it could be regarded as obstruction of justice."

The police seem to be quite capable of obstructing justice on their own. But she keeps this to herself.

Mr. Ormiston's attention remains focused on the road, but he adds: "And I still can't believe that Sophia, I mean Miss Alderman — or, whatever her name really is — could be involved in murder."

Nor can she. Was the tear in her eye after the violin performance simply more theatre? "It's circumstantial evidence, but does seem to suggest a connection between her and the attack," she says.

They continue without speaking until they approach her street.

"What are you looking for?" Mr. Ormiston asks as she climbs out of the car.

"I'll know when I find it."

It is still early and the neighbourhood is only just waking up. Her house is now cordoned off by yellow tape. For the second time in a week, she lifts the tape that reads "Police line: Do not cross", and steps past it.

She unlocks the front door and goes inside. The police completed their investigation and sealed the house, but it is clear that something has changed. The entranceway once more shows the mark of a chair that has been placed under the light fitting, even though someone has tried to fluff the carpet back up with their fingers. Above her, the matchstick camera and its cord are gone.

As she moves down the hallway to the living room, an echo of the dread she felt last night runs through her body; an alien sensation, then and now.

It is a myth that police draw chalk outlines of bodies. Apart from the fact that it would contaminate the crime scene, photographs from different angles more than suffice once the site has been examined. In any case, although Father's body has been removed she can still visualise precisely where it lay, fingers outstretched to Mother's as they lingered on opposite sides of the Styx.

Though nothing else has been disturbed, the camera here is missing also. As is the one in the dining room. She climbs the stairs to her room, knowing before she opens the doors that that camera too has been removed.

She looks for evidence of other cameras or changes in the house, but whoever returned for them has been careful. There is no evidence of forced entry. Even the residual adhesive from the tape has been removed from the various surfaces—a faint smell of ethanol suggests that this was done with rubbing alcohol. Recently.

She goes back to her parents' bedroom. The night before, she restored the underwear drawer to its prior state, wiping away the scarlet drops that came off her hand. It appears untouched, but it is the painting and what lies behind it that she has come to examine. On the wall, the pastoral scene looks the same, but a closer inspection of the frame shows that it is too clean. Mother's routine was — Mother's routine is to dust on weekends. This wood has recently been wiped down.

In case there are any fingerprints to be found, she takes a pen from the dresser to nudge the painting aside and enter the code — her birthdate — to open her parents' safe. The chirping sequence of beeps is followed by the click of the internal lock opening. Again using the pen, she swings the door open and looks inside. The family's passports are still there, along with several hundred pounds in cash and a few pieces of Mother's more precious jewellery. But something is missing.

The diaries. There were three diaries tied up with ribbon. When she opened the safe on Saturday she was looking for the stationery Mother used for the weekly puzzles, but now she pictures the diaries: brown leather notebooks tied in a bundle with purple ribbon. She did not look at them closely, but they appeared old and well-used. The leather was worn at the corners, the edges of the paper yellowed with time.

She does not recall Mother keeping a diary. When she saw them she assumed that they were a sentimental keepsake of an earlier period in her life, perhaps from her courtship with Father. Father himself is highly unlikely to have written a diary, and certainly not to have bound it in purple ribbon to keep next to Mother's jewellery.

It was improbable that Mother would have moved the diaries in the past week herself. Yet it was also improbable that a thief would break in and guess the code, ignoring the cash and jewellery, just to take her notebooks. She closes the safe once more, locking it and replacing the painting.

Returning downstairs she closes up the house and is almost at Mr. Ormiston's car when she sees Mrs. Pike walking towards her, the bulldog Winston straining ahead on his lead.

"Good morning, Mrs. Pike."

"You're back again, are you?" she says, concern written across her face. "How's your ma doing? We saw them racing her off in that ambulance last night, but I never got a chance to ask you."

"She's stable, but in a coma. We're not sure what will happen."

"Oh, dear me, that's terrible." She shakes her head. "And your poor pa. Such a nice man. I'm so sorry, Arcadia." She is lost in memories of her own for a moment before she looks up. "I did speak to that nice police officer last night, told him all that I saw."

"Thank you, Mrs. Pike. What did you tell him?"

"Oh, about the man who walked up to your place last night. Big tall fella, wearing a hat. Now you don't see many men wearing hats these days. That should be a clue right there."

A simple disguise, more likely, to shield his face from

view. But she nods for the woman to continue. "Did you see what colour hair he had, anything else about him?"

"Well, with that hat you couldn't see too much but it didn't look like he had a lot of hair — there was nothing poking out from under it. Why maybe he wore the hat because he was bald! Men can be so self-conscious about those things. And he carried an umbrella, even though there wasn't even a hint of rain." She bends down to give Winston's ears a scratch. "He was inside for an hour or so, and then walked out, calm as you like. Walked off back down the street. I'm sorry that I didn't get a proper look at his face. You know, come to think of it, that hat was pulled down kind of low."

"Did you see if he smoked a cigarette?"

"Cigarette? No, I don't think so. Filthy habit. My Winston can't bear smoke and I keep him away from people who do." The asthmatic bulldog gets another rub. "I'm sorry I can't tell you more. If I'd have known what devilry he was up to I would have called the police myself." She is beginning to cry. "It's such an awful business, dear Arcadia."

She finds herself in the odd position of having to comfort the older woman. "I'll be OK, Mrs. Pike. But tell me, did you see anything else last night or this morning, after the police left?"

Mrs. Pike wipes her eyes. "No, no. Just you is all. Anyway, Winston and I have finished our trip to the park so I'd best be getting him his breakfast. If there's anything I can do for you, Arcadia, just let me know?"

"Of course, Mrs. Pike," she says. "And thank you again."

The cigarette — the lack of a cigarette — is odd. But perhaps, like the hat and the umbrella, it is a diversion rather than a clue. Distracting attention away from that which might actually identify the killer.

"Are you sure you want to go back to school?" Mr. Ormiston asks before starting the car.

"Yes," she says. "Just to get some books and things. I can take a bus and be back at the hospital by lunch."

It is a short drive and Mr. Ormiston drops her at the main entrance. He tells the security guards that Arcadia will be leaving the school grounds early to visit her Mother in hospital. "As for me," he says, "I need to go home and shower. I don't have classes until after Friday morning prayers. You could do with a wash yourself." He writes down his mobile number on a slip of paper and passes it to her. "Call me if I can help in any way."

"You've been extremely kind, Mr. Ormiston," she says when they part, offering her hand.

Mr. Ormiston takes it. "Good luck, Arcadia."

She waves as the Jaguar disappears.

It is still early and the boys and girls of the Priory School are just stirring when she gets to the dormitory. It probably is a good idea to take a shower and clear her mind, changing clothes before heading back to the hospital.

She is climbing the stairs to the fourth storey, on which the girls' rooms are located, when she meets Henry on his way down to breakfast.

"Morning, Arcadia," he says then stops, puzzled. "Did you sleep in your clothes?"

"I'm afraid that I didn't get much sleep. My parents— my parents were in a very bad accident. I'm getting changed and going back to the hospital."

"I'm so sorry. Are they going to be OK?"

He will find out eventually, but a sudden weariness comes over her. She does not have the energy to explain the affair and simply says: "I hope so."

Another student bounds down the stairway and they step to one side to let him pass. Their elbows touch. "If you need anything," Henry is saying, "please tell me?"

"I will."

He is used to her need for occasional solitude and seems to sense that the conversation is over. He nods and continues downstairs. Less than a minute later, however, she receives a text message. From Henry. It simply says:

Sorry abt yr parents, A. Hope u feel better.
H

She smiles. Of course Henry is more than an acquaintance. Only a friend would text when he could have turned around and caught up with her, but wants to respect her need for privacy. Or perhaps he just wanted to use his phone before it has to be switched off during the school day. Or perhaps he was so used to using the phone that he texted rather than walk a few yards.

She freezes.

Pulling out the slip of paper, she dials the number Mr. Ormiston gave her. The teacher picks up after three rings. "Hang on, I'm pulling over. Who is this?"

"It's Arcadia, Mr. Ormiston."

"My goodness, that was quick. You're almost as bad as Sophia—Miss Alderman."

"She would use a phone instead of walking down a corridor?"

"She would phone instead of raising her voice," he replies. "What's this all about, Arcadia?"

"Mr. Ormiston, at last night's staff meeting. You said Miss Alderman and Headmaster were both there. Did Headmaster leave early?"

The phone is silent. "Why, yes he did. There were contractors down at the rugby pitch and then he had a fundraising dinner to go to. Arcadia, you don't think—"

In the classroom yesterday she assumed that Miss Alderman was calling someone outside school. A fundamental error. Plus the typewriter. A swirling signature. Mud. The hat and a few stray locks. And all the rest, distraction. "I'm afraid I do, Mr. Ormiston. I have to go." She hangs up.

She walks briskly across the quadrangle. As she unlocks the door to the staff wing of the administration building, she hits 'send' on her phone, a one-word text message to Magnus: "Headmaster."

It is only seconds before the reply comes: "Don't be rash." But as she has already reached the top of the stairs it is a little too late for that.

"Good morning, Miss Bennett," she says brightly to Headmaster's secretary.

Miss Bennett looks up, surprised to see a student in so early. She has also come from the staff wing rather than the general office stairs.

"I must say," she continues, before Miss Bennett can challenge her, "that is a lovely typewriter on your desk. Rare to see the old originals these days." She can hear voices behind the door. It muffles them, but clearly a man and a woman.

"It's an antique," Miss Bennett says proudly. "But we still use it for the occasional form or if Headmaster wants to type a special note to someone."

"I can imagine," Arcadia says admiringly. The voices in the office are getting heated. "Speaking of Headmaster, he asked to see me. I'll let myself in."

She is at the door before Miss Bennett can rise from her seat. "Wait, you can't just barge in there he's with —"

"Miss Alderman?" Arcadia says, opening the door.

She has entered in the middle of an argument. Both Headmaster and Miss Alderman are standing in the centre

of the room, their faces visibly strained. The tension in the air is palpable, but both turn to face her. Upon seeing her, Headmaster's face first registers surprise; Miss Alderman's seems to register concern—but Arcadia now discounts her ability to read the woman's emotions.

"That will be all, Miss Bennett," says Headmaster, taking charge of the situation after a pause. "Please go to Friday morning prayers. I may be delayed, in which case ask Mr. Roundhay to begin without me." His secretary withdraws, shutting the door. He turns to Arcadia, smoothing his white hair. Composing himself. "I was terribly sorry to hear about your parents, Arcadia. You must be devastated."

Silver-tongued to the end.

"Yes, I suppose I must be," she says. "To have your parents ripped from you—even adopted parents—is a terrible thing."

Headmaster and Miss Alderman are calibrating their responses. They know that she knows something, but not how much.

"Mother is, however, stable."

"Why, what a relief that must be," says Headmaster expansively. "But I understand that she remains unconscious."

"That's true." She looks down. She does not have Miss Alderman's acting experience, but she can try. "She did manage to say a few words, however."

"Really?" Despite himself, Headmaster takes a half-step backward.

"Yes," she looks him in the eye. "Curiously, she was asking for you. 'Mr. Milton', she said, a couple of times."

"How odd," is all that Headmaster says.

"How odd indeed." Wistfully: "Perhaps her last thought, as she lay on the brink of death, was to thank you for looking after her children so well."

"Yes." He is being careful. "Perhaps that was it."

"Or perhaps she was saying something more."

"Arcadia," Miss Alderman interjects. "This is surely a difficult time for you and your family. Maybe you should leave and be with them." Does she know where this line of conversation is going? Arcadia no longer cares.

"One thing I noticed about your school, Headmaster," she says, moving towards the bookshelf with *Nineteen Eighty-Four* on it, "is that it has cameras in virtually every room—except this one. Almost the entire campus can be watched from here, but no one watches the watcher. It's a shame, I think. Because cameras can be very useful. They help capture an objective reality. They often fail utterly, of course, to record the full context, the lived experience. But as proof that you were at my parents' house last night, for example, they would probably suffice."

"What in God's name are you talking about?" Headmaster blusters. He seems genuinely confused. He does not know about the cameras. "You are clearly delusional. I shall send for Nurse immediately." He picks up the phone.

"The cigarette threw me, I confess," she continues. "A predictable distraction for someone who has been studying too many kinds of tobacco. You collected it from an ashtray perhaps. Mr. Pratt, I recall, smokes Lucky Strikes—but his stay in hospital may cure him of that." She looks at Miss Alderman, but butter would not melt in her mouth. "I am, however, fairly confident that the mud on our doorstep will match the mud in the rugby field. Then it's a matter of checking your boots for the same mud." She returns her gaze to Headmaster, who has put the phone down without dialling.

"You were clever, almost too clever. The ruse of smashing a window in the backdoor briefly fooled the police, but as a backup you had also disguised yourself. Hiding your car out of sight. Walking with an umbrella and a hat. Giving any witness two things to notice that would not actually identify you.

"But you were rushed. You panicked. You had mud on your shoes. The window was clearly smashed after the act of violence was committed. The table showed that a guest had been invited in for whisky. And you dripped my parents' blood in the hallway.

"Nevertheless, the lack of hair did throw me. What witness could fail to notice that mane of white hair of yours? And then I realised that of course it is a wig. I wonder how you explained that to my parents when you went to see them. Perhaps you used it to come across as vulnerable. Non-threatening. When you were anything but."

Headmaster has unconsciously raised a hand to straighten a stray hair. His face is calm, but he is thinking, calibrating his next move.

"And what about the weapon. It was a very sharp blade, long and thin. The police didn't find one at the scene. You could have disposed of it, I suppose, but then there's always the chance that it will be found. Far better to hide it in plain sight, where no one would suspect. A metal blade that could be cleaned and left in place, something like a gold-plated letter opener."

She keeps her eyes on them as both Headmaster and Miss Alderman turn to the desk, where the golden blade sits next to a stack of papers. As they turn back to face her, their eyes meet. Are they still together on this? Were they ever?

"Well, what an interesting little story you have constructed!" says Headmaster, walking around behind his desk to the window. "And yet you are a little young to be setting yourself up as a police officer, don't you think?"

"The only thing I don't understand is why," she says. "What was it you asked of them? What did they refuse to do that led you to kill them?"

Headmaster turns to the window. "It's getting a little stuffy in here, don't you think?" He opens the wide glass panes that look out over the quadrangle, letting in the morning breeze. He takes two deep breaths.

"It's such a shame," Headmaster says at last. "You are at

a crucial stage of your development. I just needed Louisa and Ignatius's cooperation." His voice hardens. "And they would not cooperate."

"What did you ask them to do?"

"They were holding you back, Arcadia. I had to set you free. Your finding out that you were adopted was serendipitous—a happy coincidence, as you needed to be cut loose from their sentimentality. I had been pressing them for years that you should not be wasting your weekends with them, but your 'mother' insisted. And now she was having second thoughts about the next stage of your education. I'm afraid that couldn't be allowed."

"Is that why the envelopes that you had been preparing for her end after this week?"

Headmaster is momentarily pleased. "The envelopes? Ah, see, you are so many steps ahead of your so-called 'parents'! Yes, the envelopes were as much as she would agree to continue your training on weekends. She wanted it to be a game, a puzzle. But you are capable of so much more. And now you have worked out that the code for this weekend was to mark the transition from their guardianship to mine."

"Your guardianship?"

"Yes. Louisa and Ignatius were inferior intellects. I had always felt that it was a mistake to place you with them, but I was overruled. Now there was a chance to right that mistake. Don't you see that this was necessary if you were to develop—that if you stayed with them it would forever retard your growth?"

"And so to help me grow, you kill my parents?"

"I didn't kill your parents. I liberated you from the straightjacket of their mediocrity. They wanted you to have a 'normal' childhood. But you are not *normal*. And you could be extraordinary!"

"You're insane."

"Insane? I have spent my life crafting an environment to bring the most out of children. Raising them better than their parents ever could. To *be* better than their parents ever could be. There are costs — there are always costs. To do it scientifically, to do it objectively, means not becoming attached, not becoming biased. *I* make that sacrifice. And sometimes others must be sacrificed: parents who stunt their children, limit their potential."

There is a wild-eyed quality to Headmaster's appearance now, strange in someone who has always come across as so calm, so measured. She knows there is the real possibility of violence, but does not even consider fleeing.

"You — you, however, were special. You showed real potential from before you even enrolled at the Priory School. Your brother had gifts, but he is congenitally indolent. We made mistakes with him, mistakes that were rectified in your case. A half-scholarship to make you strive; enemies to make you fight. And look at what we have achieved! Here you stand, on the cusp of greatness."

Magnus also. Sebastian's part in this. Provocation protocols. But the delusions of the crazed man before

her do not detract from the moral simplicity of the situation. She takes out her mobile phone. "I'm phoning the police."

Headmaster's face now darkens. "You stand on the cusp of greatness—and yet your self-righteousness is insufferable. Rather than grasp this nettle, you slink off back to normality. How pathetic. But this is not how my career ends," Headmaster continues, moving away from the open window, speaking to Miss Alderman now as much as to her. "I'm not taking the fall for this. You were part of it, 'Sophia'—or whatever you're calling yourself now. You were all part of it."

"Not this," Miss Alderman says quietly. "Not murder."

"It wasn't murder," he snorts. "It was science. I thought you understood that."

"I'm not sure I understand anything anymore," the substitute teacher says, almost to herself, watching him move across the room. "You have crossed about half-a-dozen lines here, Charles. There will be consequences."

"Consequences? Bah. In any case, I think it's time we bring this experiment to an end. For if I go, you go with me." He now has his back to the door—the only exit. "I have a better idea, however. A better story. A grief-stricken Arcadia Greentree, distraught over the loss of her parents, runs to her Headmaster's office with all sorts of wild accusations. Headmaster tries to reason with her, but the girl is inconsolable. She becomes self-destructive. In a fit of misery and rage she throws herself from the Headmaster's window onto the paving stones below. A tragic end to a promising life. The school declares a half-day holiday. And then life goes on."

She enters the emergency services number, 999, into her phone.

Wild-eyed has been replaced by menacing as Headmaster now begins to advance towards her. Exit is impractical. The door is blocked, the window too high. The secret office is nearby but a dead end. Fight rather than flight, then. Boxing skills are of limited use against a far taller and heavier opponent. A weapon is needed. She turns to the desk for the letter opener, but it is gone. And with a flash of gold she sees that it is in Miss Alderman's hand.

In her own hand, she hears the number ring once, twice.

"As I said earlier, Arcadia," Miss Alderman says, her eyes on Headmaster, "it might be time for you to leave. Charles, I think you should move away from the door so that she can go, and then you and I can talk in private."

"Have you lost your mind?" Headmaster laughs. "There's no way you come out of this untouched. You're an accessory to murder, you do realise that don't you?"

"There are worse things than prison, Charles." Miss Alderman moves towards Headmaster, the blade of the paper knife pointed at his throat. "Too many people have worked too hard on this for you to throw it all away to save your own skin."

"Bah," Headmaster scoffs, but moving backwards slowly away from her. "I don't care what your professor

does to me."

The operator at the other end of the line picks up: "Emergency, which service do you require? Fire, police or ambulance?"

"No one's going to do anything to you, Charles. You're going to do it all yourself." The substitute teacher keeps her eyes on Headmaster, but says to Arcadia: "Now leave."

The door is clear but she lingers. "What are you going to do?" she asks.

"I'm going to try to make amends," Miss Alderman says. "And then I'm going to disappear." For a moment, she looks the girl in the eye: "I'm sorry, Arcadia. I hope that one day you can forgive me." For a second time, she sees a tear in Miss Alderman's eye. But it is quickly wiped away.

She, Arcadia, is next to the door and puts her hand on the knob. Through her phone she can hear the operator asking again which service she requires. Yet she knows it may be the last time she sees the substitute teacher. "Miss Alderman," she says. "The rhesus monkeys who never had a mother from birth were permanently damaged. What happened to the monkeys whose mothers were taken away later on?"

Miss Alderman keeps her attention on Headmaster, but considers her reply. "They suffered," she says at last. "But if the mother had done her job, then they dealt with it. And they got on with their lives. They survived. And so will you. Goodbye, Arcadia."

"I don't even know your real name."

"You'll find it."

Headmaster has begun to see how perilous his situation is. He now calls to his student: "Miss Greentree, please. You can see that she's crazy. Pick up the phone. Call for help—get the police. Do something. I wasn't thinking earlier—of course I would never hurt you, a student. Please!"

"I'm sorry, Headmaster," she says coldly. "But as you said earlier: I don't work for the police. I'm lucky if they even consult me."

Arcadia Greentree opens the door and walks down the empty stairs. She hangs up the call and puts the phone in her pocket, not looking back as the door slams behind her.

12
BEGINNINGS

Father's funeral service takes place the following Monday, in the church at which he and Mother were married nearly three decades earlier. It is an austere building, but stained glass windows scatter dappled light across the rows of mostly empty pews. Father's sister, Jean, and her husband, Arthur, have arranged a simple ceremony for family and friends. Some colleagues from Father's practice attend, along with a few of his patients. In all there are around two score in the congregation.

She is seated in the front row, with Magnus and their aunt and uncle. Before the altar is the coffin, the wooden box that holds what was once her Father.

They rise to sing the opening hymn, John Bunyan's "To Be a Pilgrim":

Who would true valour see,
Let him come hither...

A few rows back, Mr. Ormiston has taken the afternoon off in order to be present. He has brought her violin from school — a thoughtful gesture. They have not spoken since Friday, when she hung up on him in mid-sentence. After that brief exchange he telephoned the police, urging them to get to the Priory School as quickly as possible.

By the time Inspector Bradstreet and Constable Lestrange arrived, she was walking across the quadrangle towards the dormitory. "We're here to interview Mr. Milton, the Headmaster," Lestrange said. "Have you seen him recently?"

She was about to reply when a cry rang out from the top floor of the administration building. The police officers turned away from her to look up to the open windows of Headmaster's office — just in time to see the body as it fell down and crashed onto the paving stones below. The two men ran over to where it lay, but there was nothing to be done. Headmaster's mane of white hair had detached during the fall; caught in a breeze, the wig wafted down to land on the grass some yards away.

The officers then rushed to his office, but it was empty. She found out later that on the large oak desk there was a note written in Headmaster's swirling cursive. In it, he confessed to the murder of Ignatius and the attempted murder of Louisa Greentree. He had gone to their house with the intention of extorting money from them, he wrote, but they had refused. He had acted alone. In order to spare his family from disgrace and to limit the damage

to the school that he loved, he was choosing to take his own life. He apologised to all those he had hurt.

The suicide note was affixed to the desk by a golden letter opener, stuck almost an inch deep into the wood. It was later determined to be the murder weapon.

Her family is perhaps the least wealthy at the school, so the idea that Headmaster would choose them for the purposes of extortion makes little sense. But the police have not asked her for her views and she does not see the need to offer them. After interviewing Miss Bennett, the secretary, they began searching for Miss Alderman. Her office was found to have been hastily cleared and her apartment was deserted. They will not have much success finding her.

Today, Constable Lestrange is attending the funeral in his personal capacity — another kind gesture. It is the first time she has seen him out of uniform. Plainclothes suits him.

He is seated next to Mr. Ormiston. Earlier in the day it was announced that Mr. Ormiston is taking over as Acting Headmaster of the Priory School. A proper search will be undertaken in due course for a new Head; in the meantime, classes need to be taught and 507 boys and girls need to be fed and sheltered. His role is primarily that of a caretaker, but word has quickly spread about the surveillance network at school and Mr. Milton's secret office. Mr. Ormiston has already announced that the school will be taking down all cameras except those around its perimeter. The footage that is recorded will be held by an office of campus security and accessed only when clear need can be demonstrated.

At the front of the church, the priest announces the first reading, from Psalm 23. Magnus stands and moves to the lectern.

> Yea, though I walk through the valley of the
> shadow of death, I will fear no evil: for thou art
> with me; thy rod and thy staff they comfort me…

She and Magnus did meet, a little later than planned, on Friday afternoon at Mother's hospital bed. Mother remains in a coma and, though the doctors did not tell them so, each passing day makes it less likely that she will recover fully. But there is hope.

Over the weekend, they maintained a kind of vigil by her bedside, mostly wordless. It is the longest time that the siblings have spent together in years. Mother would have been pleased.

On Sunday, when an orderly asked them to step out of Mother's room in order to bathe her, they stood in the corridor and were nudged into conversation.

"Magnus," she said at last, "have you ever come across the term 'provocation protocol'?"

She was loath to admit ignorance in front of her brother, but her own research had been of limited success. It was possible that his access to classified government files

would yield something more. Among other things, it had turned up the warning about the threat to their parents that ultimately saved Mother's life.

"Where did you come across that term?" he responded lightly. Perhaps too lightly — subtlety was never his strong suit. But it was not the time for criticism.

"It was in the fragment of the letter that I found in Milton's secret office."

Magnus paused for only a fraction of a second, clearly determining how much to reveal. "It's a kind of experiment," he said. "A controlled way of challenging the emotional mood of an individual to determine his or her psychological stability. A way of testing the balance between one's rational brain and one's emotions — what Freud called the ego and the id. Some of our government agencies use it to evaluate agents."

"Does that suggest that Milton was connected to one of those agencies?"

"Not necessarily. Merely that there may be an overlap in the procedures." Magnus was choosing his words carefully, though he always does.

"I assume there is some connection between these procedures and academic research into the area?"

"Naturally," he said. "There is a rich field of research on how humans respond to stress and other stimuli. The ethical and legal limits on such research mean that some related work is carried out using monkeys, though even that can be controversial if the animals are seen to be treated cruelly. Why?"

"It may not have been a formal title, but at one point Milton said to Miss Alderman that he didn't care what 'her professor' did to him."

"Curious."

"That was what I thought."

"Allow me to look into the matter further."

They returned soon after to Mother's bedside, until visiting hours were over.

Magnus finishes his reading and the priest announces the second piece of scripture, from the third chapter of Ecclesiastes, which she is to read. She stands and approaches the lectern.

To every thing there is a season, and a time to every purpose under the heaven:

A time to be born, and a time to die...

Towards the back of the congregation, she sees that Henry Stamford has taken a seat. He gives her a brief thumbs up; without pausing in the reading she offers a slight nod by way of acknowledgment.

She has been offered leave of absence from the Priory School, though she has already decided that she will

continue attending classes. For the first time, she will attend as a full-boarder. When term ends for the long vacation, she will go to stay with Aunt Jean and Uncle Arthur, who are likely to become her guardians.

She has already been back to the Priory School once, briefly, on Saturday. While collecting more clothes and books she bumped into Henry, who was shocked by the events. By that time the news had permeated through the school and was being picked up by the local press. Her own role in the identification of Milton as the murderer has not emerged, however. She chooses to keep it that way.

"I still can't believe Headmaster would do such a thing," Henry remarked as they walked across the quadrangle together. "It seems completely impossible."

"Not impossible," she corrected. "Only improbable. Impossible things can be eliminated. But when you have done that, whatever remains, however improbable, must be the truth."

They reached the gate where a taxi was waiting to take her back to the hospital. Henry was on the point of saying something in response, but the driver tapped on his horn to hurry her up. Henry, her friend, opened the car door for her.

He waved until the car turned the corner and a dry stone wall blocked her from his sight.

A time to kill, and a time to heal; a time to break down, and a time to build up…

She continues the reading, her eyes moving across the congregation. She has met a few of Father's colleagues but only a handful of the patients—those tended to be the ones who visited around Christmas to drop off gifts or pay their respects. Some carry the evidence of the ailment that brought them to see Father, others would require closer examination. Even from where she stands it is relatively simple to identify those who drove or took public transport, those who work in offices or with their hands, those whose finances are stable and those who have fallen on hard times.

Standing at the back of the church is a woman, clad in black. A large-brimmed hat shields her face, but her shoulders and her posture betray her. Magnus is yet to admit defeat, but the only information that he has thus far discovered about Miss "Sophia Alderman" is that her entire digital record is a fiction. Why she would go to such elaborate lengths—including conducting a year-long affair—in order to get close to the school and to Arcadia remains unclear.

> A time to weep, and a time to laugh; a time to mourn, and a time to dance…

The woman's head is bowed, but for a moment she looks up and they make eye contact. Arcadia is wary of leaping to unfounded conclusions, but her presence is irrational unless there is some kind of connection between

them. If her intention is merely to monitor the event, there are safer ways of doing so; if Arcadia wished to apprehend "Miss Alderman", she could stop the reading and call to Lestrange to arrest her.

She does not.

A time to cast away stones, and a time to gather stones together; a time to embrace, and a time to refrain from embracing...

The Bible verse she has committed to memory, but she must look down to turn the page. In the fraction of a second that her attention is focused on the lectern, the woman withdraws, a slight movement of the west door to the church the only evidence of her presence. It closes as she concludes the reading:

A time to rend, and a time to sew; a time to keep silence, and a time to speak;
A time to love, and a time to hate; a time of war, and a time of peace.

Her Aunt Jean, Father's sister, delivers the eulogy. She recounts stories from the different periods of his life, touching on the alcoholism of his own father and Ignatius's struggles with his faith. Tales from his medical studies in Edinburgh are greeted with knowing smiles and an occasional laugh from his fellow practitioners.

On his wife and children, Aunt Jean is brief. Ignatius first met Mother as one of his patients, whom he then got to know socially. They brought each other happiness and comfort; the pride that they felt for their son and their daughter was without limit.

Listening to her, Arcadia recalls their last conversation, in the car park at school after the concert. Father, out of concern for Mother's health, had asked her to wait until the weekend to discuss her adoption. There will be time enough, he had said. Yet he was wrong. Time ran out.

And then the service is over. As a final hymn is sung the pallbearers are asked to come forward. Three medical practitioners stand on one side; Arthur, Magnus, and she on the other. Custom usually limits pallbearers to male friends and relatives, but she was firm. The six pause beside the coffin and then raise it to their shoulders.

Later, they will drive to the cemetery to lay Father's remains in the ground. There will be a small reception and then the immediate family members will return to the hospital where Mother lies.

If Mother wakes, answers to the questions that remain unanswered may be forthcoming. But in the meantime she will begin her own investigations into the identity of the woman Sophia Alderman, the professor to whom she referred, and the person who broke into their home to

install and then remove the surveillance cameras, as well as steal Mother's diaries.

The police regard the case as closed.

But the police, she now knows, have limits to their imagination and their powers of deduction. She does not put herself in their place—she has no desire to supply their deficiencies. Nevertheless, she resolves to carry the matter further, wherever it may lead, to find out not just what happened to her parents, but why.

They reach the doors of the church, held open by two ushers. As she steps into the air outside, an east wind picks up, scattering some leaves across their path and a few stray pieces of confetti from a recent wedding.

Father's coffin is not heavy on her shoulder, but she becomes aware of a stinging sensation in her eye. Perhaps a stray piece of confetti has blown into it. She raises her free hand to remove it and her finger comes away wet, dampened by the single tear that she has stopped before it could make its way down towards her cheek.

Arcadia Greentree will return in
FINDING ARCADIA

To understand the present, Arcadia Greentree must dig into her past.

Her father murdered and her mother in a coma, Arcadia tries to locate the "professor" whom she believes to be ultimately responsible. A series of clues lead her to Oxford University and a confrontation with her enemy—but all is not as it seems.

ABOUT THE AUTHOR

 **SIMON CHESTERMAN** is a Professor and Dean of the National University of Singapore Faculty of Law. Educated in Melbourne, Beijing, and Oxford, he has lived and worked for the past decade in Singapore. He and his wife have two children, who are voracious readers. Simon is the author or editor of seventeen books, including *One Nation Under Surveillance, Just War or Just Peace?* and *You, The People*. This is his first novel and the only one of his books that his children have read voluntarily.